D0445472

THE TAKING OF
JAKE LIVINGSTON

THE TAKING OF

JAKE LIVINGSTON

RYAN DOUGLASS

G. P. PUTNAM'S SONS

G. P. PUTNAM'S SONS
An imprint of Penguin Random House LLC, New York

Copyright © 2021 by Ryan Douglass Williams

G. P. Putnam's Sons is a registered trademark of Penguin Random House LLC.

Visit us online at penguinrandomhouse.com

Library of Congress Cataloging-in-Publication Data
Names: Douglass, Ryan, author.
Title: The taking of Jake Livingston / Ryan Douglass.
Description: New York: G. P. Putnam's Sons, 2021. | Summary: "When a
murderous ghost begins to haunt sixteen-year-old Jake Livingston, high school
soon becomes a different kind of survival game"—Provided by publisher.
Identifiers: LCCN 2021004834 (print) | LCCN 2021004835 (ebook) |
ISBN 9781984812537 (hardcover) | ISBN 9781984812544 (ebook)
Subjects: CYAC: Mediums—Fiction. | Ghosts—Fiction. | Survival—Fiction.
Classification: LCC PZ7.1.D682 Tak 2021 (print) | LCC PZ7.1.D682 (ebook) |
DDC [Fic]—dc23
LC record available at https://lccn.loc.gov/2021004834
LC ebook record available at https://lccn.loc.gov/2021004835

Manufactured in Canada
ISBN 9781984812537

1   3   5   7   9   10   8   6   4   2

Design by Suki Boynton
Text set in Kepler Std

For everyone fighting a silent battle.

JAKE

I'd hate to be that kid who died in PE class.

Steven Woodbead never saw it coming. He was body-rolling to a trap song when the javelin hit his skull.

He died on the spot. Went splat in the grass, with the javelin sticking out of his forehead like the sword of King Arthur. According to St. Clair lore, a few people were screaming "LOOK OUT!" even as his hand unraveled like the legs of a dead crab and his portable speaker rolled slowly from his grip. Woodbead is dead, but I can still see him, bursting into light when the javelin lands.

Steven is deader than dead, and he died before I was even born. His PE uniform—white crop top and blue shorts—doesn't match the all-red uniforms we wear today and definitely wouldn't be considered "normal" by the academy's current standards. Any dude wearing a shirt that doesn't cover his belly button would have their face shoved into an unflushed toilet. So I assume Steven died in the eighties. All I can see is the moment his soul split from his body—when his shirt knifed open and firecrackers burst like bees from his chest. His body dispersed in a siege of glowing embers, disintegrating into the air around the rugby post. There's this moment afterward when that spot is silent, and at first I wondered if that was his final loop, if Steven had finally passed on. But then he pixelates back into shape, short shorts to retro windbreaker. His smile is empty, his eyes are white, and he's dancing all over again.

"Jake!" Grady's voice whistles through the air like a firework behind me. "Wait up!"

Can't talk right now. Too busy watching Woodbead blow up, hoping he'll be done with that awful business soon. In the year I've been at this school, I've noticed his body parts slowly fading. Three fingers of his left hand have already dissolved, and his right leg ends just below the knee.

The ancient brick castle of my school fades into view. We're passing the tennis courts and running toward the start line, where the wide steps lead back to campus. Turning the corner ahead of us are our top athletes—Chad Roberts and Laura Pearson, who, in their all-red uniforms, look like moving blood cells with pale appendages.

"Jake!" Grady falls in line next to me, head all sweaty. "Um, earth to Jake?"

"Oh. Hi, Grady."

He's the only friend I have here, for better or worse. He's three inches shorter than me, with a white face and bushy orange hair. "You trying to ditch me, man? I've been calling you for twenty minutes!"

"Have you?"

"You're always so damned zoned out."

Our voices are pitched so differently. Mine is subdued and so quiet you can barely hear it. His is nasal and shrill—too loud to tune out.

Our friendship never really settled in—it's actually a long-lasting accident, which started at the courtyard tables last year, when he invited himself to sit next to me. I was reading. He asked me what I was reading. My solitude ended, and I've never gotten it back.

A whistle shrieks from the field. Coach Kelly's got his blue eyes set on me. His neck is stiff, and the bill of his hat hides the top half of his face. He's pumping his arms in slow motion, pantomiming proper running. It's so condescending.

I hate it here. Every time we run warm-up laps it's like there's a BLACK KID sign blinking above my head like a firetruck light, alerting the coaches of my whereabouts on the track. They are always keeping their eyes on me. Most days I want to run off this campus, find shelter in the woods, and spend a few years not being perceived, just to recover from the trauma of being hyper-visible.

And most days? I can't figure out what I hate more: seeing the dead or being the one Black eleventh grader at St. Clair Prep.

⁘

I change into my uniform in the stall of the second-floor bathroom. Here is the best place to escape from all the shirt thrashing and butt slapping of the boys' the locker room. Covering the walls are stickers for clubs I will never be a part of. Varsity Crew, Math League, St. Clair Democrats, St. Clair Republicans. They're all slapped over each other like each club is competing for dominance, forming a big psychedelic collage of red, white, and blue. All surrounding a doodle of Mr. Krabs, captioned *Krabs is one thicc bih.*

The stall door clacks behind me as I approach a sink mirror— one of three hung on a blue wall of ceramic tiles. All that it shows me is that I'm not much to look at.

On my way out of the bathroom, I hear my brother shouting.

"Give me back my shit, man!"

The hallway traffic is buzzing like a chaos of katydids. Jocks, band geeks, and loners all wear the same navy-blue blazers, sucking all the culture out of the place. You can only tell who's in what clique by the clusters that form in front of lockers and by the fact that jocks wear their blazers open.

My brother doesn't wear the blazer at all. He wears whatever he wants. I stop walking when I see him arguing with my chem teacher, Mr. Shaw, on the landing past the glass at the end of the hall.

Mr. Shaw is holding my brother's snapback out of reach. "*No hats in the building. It is against the dress code.*"

"It's *not* a hat! It's a headband. Show me where the dress code says *no headbands*, bruh."

Benji is five-eleven, but Mr. Shaw is a giant at six-five and can hold the hat higher than most people. His jacket sleeve forms a curtain that hangs over Benji's face as Benji jumps up to grab it.

It's a loud and humiliating sight, which would be worse if people actually knew that we were brothers. You couldn't guess it because Benji's heavy like a linebacker, with a warm beige skin tone and a smooth wave pattern. I'm two inches shorter, skinny as a pole, with golden-brown skin and two different hair textures—nappy on the sides, curly on top.

Mr. Shaw is guiding Benji in the direction of the principal's office as I slip into my first class. Benji's arguing the whole time, not letting it go, asserting his right to dress how he wants. Sometimes I wish I could be like him—more in charge of myself. Instead, I'm silent all the time.

✣

When Mom used to ask me what I learned in school, I couldn't tell her. I still couldn't, because it's hard to pay attention when you live in hiding at the back of the classroom.

Dead world appears around me like a subaquatic wasteland of lost matter—failed tests, rusty trophies, dismembered trumpets, and ripped baseballs. Lost memories floating through the walls, over everybody's heads, and out the other side. The phantoms blur together in a drone of chaos I've trained myself to ignore. That guy in the tweed vest who breaks the school chair over another dude's neck in chemistry. That awkward moment in econ when a car crashes through the wall and just sits there with phantom bricks like visual static on its windshield, obscuring the bloody person inside. The lights blink so bright they block the board.

I wanted classes only on the second floor to avoid proximity to roads. And the third floor is too high, because the ghosts up there jump out of windows.

I am always focused on drawing. My notebooks are filled with demented sketches that normal people would call weird. Robots with spider legs and worms crawling out of eyeballs. Eyeballs with giant bellies. A boy with a bloated, bleeding heart for a head.

The final bell brings me home. The glockenspiel does its *ding dong ding* thing, and my eyes waken to my second reality—the one where ceiling lights blast through ghosts so hard I can barely see them. And the world is replaced by kids who don't know my name.

⁜

I live in Atlanta, but not really. Clark City is too far out for the train to come, unless it's one of those freight trains crawling slowly down the tracks and forcing cars to wait five minutes for it. Clark City's half Black, a quarter white, and a quarter blend of Congolese, Eritrean, Afghan, and Vietnamese. Food trucks offer our most convenient eateries—Benton Bell's wing truck and Strong Island Caribbean Café. Houses hide behind trees, their windows boarded, roofs slogged down in moisture. Construction workers tear projects down and put more corporate things up—car dealerships and gas stations. The breaking and building never ends.

There is no crosswalk to my subdivision, so I jaywalk when the timing feels right, making it across the street just in time for a car to rip through the fog behind me, thrashing my back with cool air.

Blue lights flash in the distance, up the curve to my house, and there's caution tape stretched across a driveway. The police are talking to my neighbors—the Mooneys, I think. Their home is a plantation-style thing with a wraparound fence, dripping with fake cobwebs for Halloween. Also: fake graves in the lawn.

The middle-aged couple in navy-blue suits are lonely. They hug each other in the driveway. Her head is in his neck, and he's staring into space. A field of indigo light curls off their heads, forming a smoky field with chunks of matter like planet waste—ice and dust and tiny rocks all melting into a living thing.

A pair of ghouls hovers over them, dipping their emaciated gray heads down to suck the smoke through their spiky teeth, slit nostrils, and eyeless eyes.

Their business is none of mine. I keep pushing to my house.

There's a ringing from somewhere. No . . . screaming? Screaming and begging.

"Wait! Stop, WAIT!"

Must be coming from behind an open window, or dead world. I hear voices from the second world, like the voices that called out to warn Steven a javelin was on its way to kill him. These voices are always in distress. Sometimes they warn; sometimes they plead.

I'm cold suddenly. Summer always ends late down here, but it's officially over now, and the wind is not warm anymore. A gust of it blasts my beanie off my head, and I spin to catch it, finding myself face-to-face with a rib cage. A rib cage like . . . a giant rotisserie chicken stripped of meat.

No nipples; a stretched, long neck; and a giant head, alien-shaped, with gaping holes in place of eyes. The ghoul obscures everything behind it, but if I reached out to touch it, my hand would fade through its body. They're not real. They only look like they are.

I turn, and it follows me, like a zombie hobbling after its meal. Then I'm running up my driveway, suddenly unconvinced that it can't actually touch me. I know what I've read about the creatures, and what my medium mentor, Ms. Josette, has taught me—*They can't hurt you, because they can't touch you.*

So why does the ground shake when they walk, rattling the street pebbles? Why do the asphalt cracks look strained under their footsteps? The hatchbacks and minivans parked on the street seem worried a storm will destroy them.

The creature's horrible shadow falls over me, sinking my stomach into no-man's-land.

I'm not the one grieving, so I'd be of no interest to the leeches of dead world. They tend to avoid happy people, instead latching on to the most sullen, tragic person in the room. I've only ever grieved my dog, Appa, who died of heart failure two years ago. My family's mostly alive, except for my grandfather, who died six months before I was born. I don't think I'll ever see my dad again, but he's still alive out there.

Now there's laughter—children's laughter—and the pop of a gun.

Something terrible happened in my neighbors' house.

It's getting cold too fast, like the entire winter is dropping here and now. A shadow comes down like a blanket of ice as I search my four pockets—slacks and hoodie.

Where are my keys?

There are moments when it controls me. The shadows, the darkness. Moments where I become dizzy, undefined, just a floater like the failed tests in my classrooms.

But I know my porch—a column of white balusters. I know my front door—dead bolt and handle that you push down to get inside. A freezing wind sweeps under my hoodie, pulling me backward. I tilt my way into the house and click the door shut.

The TV's playing from the living room. Somehow. Mom's out of town.

"Benji?" I call.

No answer.

The air is cold inside, and the light is so dim that even the earth-tone prints on the wall have lost their luster.

Around the entryway, I find the TV on Channel 2 News.

"We have to put a stop to gun violence. How many more people have to die?"

There's a headline with a picture of my neighbor—the son of the weeping couple.

MATTEO MOONEY, SURVIVOR OF HERITAGE HIGH SHOOTING, FOUND DEAD IN HOME

Oh my God . . .

Matteo is . . . dead?

I don't know anybody in the neighborhood, but I did notice when Matteo moved in. Him and Mr. Mooney forced a sofa through the door. Matteo was shirtless, the shirt tucked into his back pocket. The neighbors were all spying on his sweaty jock body, his shapely pecs. The sun was a hot bubble swelling over Clark City, and the humidity made me take off my own shirt, open the window, and put the fan in it. I watched Matteo come in and out of the house, wondering how much I'd have to lift to get so big. I wanted so badly to grow over my collarbones and elbows.

I sink into the couch leather.

I remember the school shooting. The Heritage killer sent a shock wave through all of Atlanta. Everyone was paranoid because one of those things had come so close to home.

I watch a clip of Matteo speaking at a podium. It's dated a year ago, right after the shooting. Cameras flash on the tears in his eyes as he looks out over an outdoor audience. "How many more of our friends do we have to lose before we say 'enough is enough'? There are demons out there who just want the world to burn. And we have to come together to make sure they can't get the weapons to harm us."

It cuts away. Matteo's face appears side by side with the shooter who attacked his school.

Sawyer Doon. Yes, the menace with the straight blond hair and blue eyes.

The news anchors reappear, their faces molds of fake sadness. "Heartfelt words from Matteo Mooney. May he rest in peace. Our thoughts and prayers are with the Mooney family. The cause of death is currently unknown."

I turn off the TV and stand up, staring at nothing. I guess a ghost came and turned it on when I was gone.

Murder. In my neighborhood. Matteo was like . . . eighteen? Nineteen?

I slog up to my room, and the house begins to feel heavy and too silent around me, like *someone is here, something will jump out.*

No one's here. I'm in my room, turning my book bag upside down. Textbooks, pens, and worksheets fall free in a frenzy on my mattress.

I lift the blinds and watch the blue house at the end of the street. Police lights reflect in the second-story windows.

Strange. I never thought the richest kid in our community would be the one to die.

I collapse on the mattress and watch the globelike light fixture.

The final daylight surrenders to the dark trap of night. Ectomist creeps at my periphery, snakelike and sinister.

It's the matter that eats ghosts as the seasons turn, nibbling on their fading bodies, burrowing inside of them like termites. It's what makes all loops end, eventually. It's everywhere and nowhere at once, coating the carpet, thickening the air with glittering fibers.

It's always seeping in through the vents, the plumbing stacks, and cracks in the plaster like carbon monoxide, here to asphyxiate me in my sleep.

SAWYER

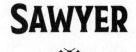

October 9

Dear Diary,

Don't know why the doctor made me do this, or who I'm even supposed to be talking to. It's too dark in the shed to even see what I'm writing. So there's no way to make sense of what I'm thinking. The lantern only shows me the center of the page. What I wrote before doesn't matter. What I write next won't either.

"Sawyer! Sawyer! Sawyer!"

Have you ever heard your name called so much that you wanted to die?

Momma must hate me. Made the doctors release me from Hapeville before I could promise Tom I'd never try to kill myself again. So I don't know if I will try again. She took me out of there a week ago because it embarrassed her to have a kid at a treatment center. I know from what Annie told me when we got home, when Momma was out of earshot: "Are you sure you're okay? Because you know they wanted to keep you in there and Momma made 'em let you go."

I pictured all Momma's coworkers at the diner judging her for not being able to answer the question "How's your son doing?"

This outhouse-turned-shed-turned-haven was where my dad kept his power tools. Momma hasn't touched it since he ditched us last September. She always asks me if I tried to off myself because he left. I think she gives him too much power.

The pine trees are so long they sneak through the crescent at the top of the door. The wallpaper in my cell at the clinic felt just as three-dimensional and murky, and I guess it reminds me of there, that place that felt more like home than here. Something about a hospital gown, a public bed, a tall dark man named Tom talking to me twice a day. He had beautiful bones in his face.

"Sawyer! Sawyer! Sawyer!" You should hear my mom yelling right now.

No one past the forest will know she's shouting. But it will annoy the shit out of my sister, who's probably in her room, writing in her own diary or messaging her mean friends.

Momma always asks me if she's a good mother. I don't know what to tell her.

She only ever started cooking for me after I tried to hang myself. She makes more sandwiches than necessary and refrigerates them for the next day, so they aren't as good when I eat them.

"SAWYER, are you out there? Please come inside and eat!"

August is over, but when it was here, you could hear all these cicadas chattering at a frequency that felt designed to shatter all sense in the brain and turn you insane. In my bedroom, I opened the screenless window and listened to their hellish roar. The terror of it.

They formed the soundscape to my process as I wrapped an extension cord around the fan.

I have never been on the same page as anyone.

I've heard the question "How's Sawyer?" more in the past week than I ever have before. Momma's always got the phone on speaker before and after work. Aunt Celia, Uncle Rod, Gramma, and even my kid cousins, Connor and Georgie, all want to know how I am.

"He's doing all right!" she says. "Gettin' lots of rest and all that good stuff."

She never even asks how I'm doing, though. She paints her nails and watches TV and brings men home every so often when she thinks we're asleep.

Uncle Rod says we should move out of the forest. "Great big world out there," he says. "Can't be stuck in Bill's bumfuck Georgia fantasy forever."

Funny how Rod is just like my dad, Bill, but thinks he is different.

"We're all adjusted here," Momma says.

I have never been adjusted and neither has she. She stares at the overflow of dirty bowls by our sink until no more can fit. Says, "You or Annie gonna take care of these dishes anytime soon?" I think she has more problems than me.

My dad had more problems than both of us put together. He slapped me in the face if I stared at him for too long. He sold prescription drugs and was a cable man. At the grocery store, when the self-checkout said "Help is on the way," he punched the screen and shouted, "I don't need it, you bitch!"

His skin looked like a graffitied skating ramp. He did improvement projects, like painting our whole house puke green. We live in a section of forest at the end of a long dirt trail. Regular wheels aren't made to weather it, but Bill liked it out here because he didn't want neighbors.

My dad was a sadist who dropped a ten-pound weight on a duck at the lake when I was five. I think he forced Momma to marry him and make a family so he could move it to the woods and then abandon it.

"Sawyer!" Momma's voice is more grating than a blender.

If she cares, she'll come and find me.

JAKE

Mom and Benji argue about everything, so I keep my earphones in all the time.

We're on our way to school, speeding some because we're late. The Tahoe passes Freedom Parkway and John Lewis Boulevard as Benji and Mom scream about . . . something. The dress code, maybe, or Benji's flopping grades.

My music selection is a slow bleed because I'm not fully awake. The Postal Service, SZA, and Syd. I'm drawing faces in the window fog—dragons and devils. A ghoul followed me home from Matteo's house yesterday. I haven't seen one of those things get so close to me since . . . well, since the first time I ever saw one like that, in my bedroom when I was ten.

Mom's getting my attention from the rearview mirror, her jet-lagged eyes doting and impatient. I pull out my earphones.

"I know you're tired of me asking," she says. "You sure you don't want to get your license?"

"I'm sure."

I look out the window. I could never trust myself on these roads, where the cars crash as often as they reach their destinations.

We arrive when everyone else is already in class. St. Clair's front lawn is so green it looks artificial. It probably is. So the trees and tulips in the big lawn out in front of the school where we stop the truck could be fake too. Maple leaves sweep the air from the brick walkways to the belfry. The stone saint on her post looks unhappier than usual to see us.

Benji gets out first and shuts the door without a word, like always.

Mom sighs. "Have a good day, Jake."

It doesn't sound all that sincere. I think his negativity rubs off on her, and then she transfers it to me.

I get out and stand there on the asphalt, watching the truck head in one direction and my brother in the other.

I'm always by myself.

Ms. Kingston is teaching when I make it to English, harping on about something I'd have been lost on even if I'd arrived on time.

She stops mid-speech when I enter, puts a hand on her angular hip, and gives me a green-eyed hate glare. "Nice of you to finally join us. Have a seat."

I steal a chair in the discussion circle next to Fiona Chan. All I really know about her is she's the one person in class who doesn't stare at me like an escaped prisoner when I get here late.

Ms. Kingston's still watching me as I unpack. "Anything you'd like to say?"

"Oh. Sorry."

She shakes dead brown hair out of her face. "Anyway. Now that everyone has *arrived*, we can turn back to our discussion.

Everyone should have read through page one hundred and nine of *The Great Gatsby*. Chad? You started our discussion last time. Who are you passing the baton to?"

Chad Roberts—he's one of those rugby dudes who can't mind his own business. Chews his gum extra loud and throws his voice in your face when he speaks. Just needs to be heard. His girlfriend, Laura Pearson, sits right next to him, doe eyes fluttering every time he makes a move.

"Uhhhhh . . ." Chad picks up the book like he's never seen one before and then slams it down. Leans back in his chair and fixates his beady blue eyes on me. "I want to hear what Livingston thought of the reading."

"Benj—" Ms. Kingston gives her head a little shake. "I'm sorry . . . *Jake*." She almost called me Benji. "Anything you found exciting or meaningful about the pages?"

Her tone is condescending, like she already knows I didn't read. Which I didn't. But not because I *can't* read, like she thinks. Just because *The Great Gatsby* is a snoozefest, and if I'm gonna read words, I'd rather them be by Octavia Butler, Tananarive Due, or Stephen Graham Jones instead of the guy who wrote a story about the tragedy of being rich.

I'm silent. Fiona raises her hand, but Ms. Kingston doesn't acknowledge it.

Ms. Kingston pivots her utterly offended frame toward me. "Have you arrived late and neglected to read as well?"

At this point, there's no denying it. "Yeah." My voice is a mumble. "Sorry."

"In that case, why don't you go and sit outside and read?" She flicks a finger at the door like she's commanding a dog. "You can spend the period catching up to the rest of us."

I'd rather not be here anyway, but it's embarrassing to have to turn my back on everyone and hear the silence crackling with judgment as I leave.

"Okay! Let's try that again."

Ms. Kingston's voice quiets as the door hisses shut.

The hallway is creepy when abandoned. Too silent and big for one person. I feel like a piece of food tossed through a giant's hungry intestine.

The ceiling lights are bright enough to rip right through my corneas, so I close my eyes. "Ah, peace," I whisper. "St. Clair's diploma will set you up nicely for a college with an impressive national ranking. Or something."

I want to be a cartoonist, but I've never thought of a degree as an important part of taking people on visual adventures. In fact, school never feels very important at all. I have no friends here—not that I had any friends at my old high school either, but this one has less fights and more potential, as Mom would say.

I open my eyes, kick a pencil across the floor, and listen to it roll. Each classroom I pass has some teacher warbling on like a robot, and I'd hate to be one of the kids in there.

A documentary drones from within a dark room. A flute creates a tune in the auditorium. Trumpets and tubas and triangles add a questlike whimsy. The intensity builds, and more instruments join. A clarinet. Drums grow in power, rising like a tempest.

A gunshot.

A gunshot?

The music collapses to a stop. More gunshots sound off.

I break for the doors and then trip, my body splashing into the floor like a spilled tray as a ringing torpedoes through my ears.

It's silent for a moment. Someone bursts from a classroom and tears down the hallway. Screams chase him from the door.

BANG!

It's empty and then overcrowded all at once. Kids tumble like zombies from classrooms, bumping into each other or falling down. I find my feet and fall against the lockers. Someone trips and falls beside me, books splattering out of her hands. I rush out to help her and a hand yanks me by the jacket and throws me into the lockers. "MOVE!"

Chad. Barreling like an ogre down the hallway, leaving us in the dust.

We've rehearsed the steps a million times. *Run. Hide. Fight.* But I can't move.

A hand meets my arm, sending my heart into my windpipe.

"Jake!" screams a voice. "We have to go!"

A girl moves past me. I follow her hair through the chaos. My wits blur across the ties and vests spilling out like ants from a disturbed hill, hands grabbing and heads bumping into backs. Our ceilings are the kind with panels that push back. I could climb on someone's shoulders, jump into the ceiling, and hide.

"Bethany?" someone screams. "BETHANY!"

Shuffling and panic, everyone screaming, running this way and that, only half-certain they're here. Kids frantically jabbing at their phones, fingers shaking, silencing them? Texting their final goodbyes?

At the end of the hall, my hands crash into the push handle of the front doors. I fly into the sunlight, plain sense returning to me in the shuffle down the steps. Tree branches sway like veins ripped from their connectors, but they're shielding a bright sun, and I'm underneath it—not trapped in that horrible school, not a victim of the shooter.

I'm alive. I'll make it home.

It's silent, and still, and cold. No police at the carpool lane. No SWAT team in the front yard. Everyone who escaped is just . . . standing around. Catching their breath with their hands on their knees, laughing, comforting their friends. As if the whole thing is already over . . . or never happened?

Principal Ross and Vice Principal Davis are standing together—one plump and one thin—as we panic and pour out. They're out of the way, but close to the school, as if there's no real danger.

Because there isn't. It was just a drill.

JAKE

The administration brings us into the auditorium for an assembly when it's over. They form a military line on the stage, with our janitor, Mr. Dao, standing off to the side. Principal Ross asks us to applaud Mr. Dao for how subtly he placed hidden speakers down the hallways and then operated the noise.

My gray-haired, hunchbacked principal walks across the stage. "Okay, Saber Cats." He's always lackluster, bored, breathing heavy. "What did we learn?"

Everyone is quiet at first. And then teachers chime in about what was done wrong or right.

Turns out everything was done right because there's no wrong answer.

What do you do when there's a shooter, anyway? You try not to panic, try to stay alive, hide in corners, board up doors with desks, and escape through doors or windows. All of it is right, as long as you are trying to stay alive.

What if my classmates were murdered?

What if, at some point, it wasn't a drill? What if they passed into the afterlife and were stuck in their death loops, dying forever? I would see my acquaintances running down hallways and staircases in terror. I would never be able to forget it, because it would be right in my face all the time.

⁘

I don't make it past the front lawn at the end of the day. I just plop on the ledge by the parking lot and roll a rose quartz stone around in my hand. It's hard to just bounce back to normal after a schoolwide panic.

"Hey, brobro, you need a ride?"

Benji. He's making his way around the ledge to meet me. No track practice today, I guess.

"Why are you just sitting there by yourself?" he asks. "Where's Grady?"

"Grady takes the bus."

"Come on—Mahalia's waiting for us."

Benji picks me up by the armpits and steers me through the parking lot.

My brother treats me like shit most of the time. Sometimes he treats me okay. I hate it when he's nice to me, because I know it won't last.

Mahalia is at the wheel when I open the door to her blue van, her hair in a ponytail of fresh microbraids. She smiles at me, face joyful and friendly, as always. "Hey, Jake."

Her skin is pretty, like polished amber, and she smells like tea and flowers. Mahalia is Benji's ex. She grew up in church with us, lives in our neighborhood, and drives her mom's car, so we hitch rides home with her when she's not tutoring or doing yearbook.

Benji gets in and instantly starts with smart comments. "Careful not to hit anybody backing out, Maha."

"All front-seat passengers must remain silent for the duration

22

of the ride," she says, rolling her eyes and adjusting the mirror. "It's the rules."

Unlike me, she claps back against my brother's sly comments. I swear he causes her more stress than necessary, even for an on-and-off couple. For some reason she puts up with it. They both put up with each other.

"Have you finished your application?" she asks Benji without looking at him.

"What application?"

"Georgia State? The one due in two months?"

"That's forever away."

"Benji, you'll get high and look up and it'll be January."

"I'll finish it in time."

"You already got rejected from your entire first round. Do you wanna be a flop forever?"

"Thanks, Maha. Appreciate you so much." Benji balls up his fist and looks out the window.

Benji's had girlfriends since the fifth grade. Mahalia's probably the one girl who stuck because she cares for him while challenging him. And she takes no shit.

I wish I had some of that quality in me or at least enough charm to attract someone who'd break up with me and then come back again.

⁘

At home, Mahalia takes a long deep breath and looks at my brother like there are words she needs to say that she can't say in front of me. He looks back at her, and I feel like a third wheel. When it's time for them to say goodbye, it's like they don't know how to when I'm around.

"Catch you later," Benji says, and leaps out of the car.

Then Maha and I are sitting there, just the two of us, sans the guy who's incredibly hard to talk to but whose approval you still seek, in a weird way.

"Sorry Benji's such an idiot," I tell her. "I'm embarrassed by it."

She laughs and then sighs, looking sadly at the steering wheel. "Aren't we all embarrassed? I just want more for him, you know? Like, why can't he be more studious, like you?"

"I'm not that studious."

"But you make an effort, at least. He's so smart and is just wasting it. Anyway . . . I hope you're okay after the craziness of today."

"I'm good. Thanks again for the ride."

"Always. Have a good night. See you tomorrow."

I get out of the car and find my brother in the driveway, squinting at me as she drives off.

"What were y'all talking about?" he asks.

"Just reassuring her at least one of us is a nice person so she doesn't feel alienated from our family entirely." I walk up the driveway, stick the key in the door, and twist. "Is Maha your number one or number three now? Kinda hard to keep track."

He reaches between me and the door and hits me in the chest before I can finish. The knob twists in my hand, and I fall against the doorway, coughing as the door swings open.

There's a smell. It's coming from inside the house, but it doesn't smell like the lavender Mom puts in the oil diffuser, or the potpourri on the entry table.

The pink-orange light of the sunset comes through the open door, capturing letters on our entryway wall.

S.A.D.

They're in dark red and sloppily written, like the work of a hateful vandal with no artistic talent. A demonic four-year-old who did an art project in someone else's house. An art project in blood. It came from a deep valve in the body that never should have been touched in the first place. It's sticky. Wiggly. Done, most likely, in the blood of some unassuming person.

I'm not breathing. My head is dizzy.

"What ... the ... fuck?" Benji is confused too.

"You see it too?"

This is not some dead object bleeding into my reality—this writing is really here. Someone wrote their initials in blood in my house. And they meant for us to find it.

SAWYER

October 14

DIARY,

My ssssssssssssssssssssssssssssssssssssssssssssister drives me nuts!!!!!!!!!!
Ican'tfuckingbreathe. I just broke our coffee table. Turned it
over in the living room, threw it right into the TV stand, made a
giant cracking noise. The glass cracked right down the middle.
I peeled Momma's books off that brown bookshelf and let them
loose behind me.

She screamed my name and ran desperately from the
kitchen.

I snatched a candleholder off the mantel and threw it at the
wall, so it stuck there, in a dent of crumbling plaster.

Momma blocked my path as I went for the other one, screech-
ing at me to stop.

Annie came running in the house, screaming too. "What the
hell is wrong with you, Sawyer?"

I was making no noise, but I was the crazy one? Tell me how
that is possible. They always say, "Come inside, Sawyer!" Like
there's a point to being indoors. Now they will see why I don't like
to be inside.

Momma hugged the vase close to her chest and turned on Annie, rightfully angry at her. "What did you DO to him?" Her voice was full of tears.

"Sawyer had dead bugs in the shed, Momma!" Annie was hysterical too, real riled up. "He tortured them to death and was just keeping them prisoner out there in old jelly jars."

My bug collection had grown exponentially. Cicadas, crickets, moths, dragonflies, butterflies, and beetles stuffed in empty jelly jars lining the walls, like potpourri, living and dead.

I escaped down the hallway to my room, letting my sister's nasal voice fade behind me. I want that voice to fade forever.

"What's that got to do with you, Annie?" Momma cried, pleading. "What's that got to do with you?"

I slammed my door, locked it, and screamed into the carpet. My room has one window, and a bed and a closet. A place to sleep, a place to hide, a place to escape.

Annie took my jars to the creek and tossed them all in. She threw out my experiments, just to destroy the one thing that brought me joy.

And they wonder why I don't want to be here. Why I don't want to live anymore.

The journaling thing. I understand it better now, and why Dr. Scott tells me to do it. It's to keep me from hurting people, which I forget I can't do. I think I tried to off myself because deep down I know I may hurt someone badly one day, and that seems unfair by normal standards.

I don't belong here.

Ceiling fan, why did you break?

I shouldn't have moved the bed out from under me. Annie only came running because there was a loud noise. I miss when they forgot about me.

I will never live this down—I will always be the boy with the breaking point.

I will miss the spiders the most.

Spiders even kill other spiders. Sometimes female spiders eat their mates while they're mating. Sometimes they eat their babies. Sometimes the babies eat the mom. They're my favorite. They mind their own space.

Momma's voice carried past the door. "What's he got to do with you?"

I hate how they say "he"—like what they mean is "it."

I used tweezers to pick legs off a daddy longlegs to determine how many it would need to survive. The answer is five, at least. With four legs taken off, it cannot survive, because half of it is missing. They cluster together and release a stinky secretion as a group when they see a predator. Clustered together, the spiders look like a big patch of hair. A single unit, unbreakable.

I am so sad.

I wish Annie were scared of the woods like Momma. I want them all to myself.

I'm not worth very much to my family, and they're not worth much to me either.

JAKE

Someone could be in our house. I'm dizzy and falling into the side table.

Benji grabs my arm and puts one finger over his lips. He leads me slowly, silently, through the passage to the kitchen.

The cabinets and drawers and oven are closed, the countertops just as we left them, with the mail cascading in a chaos ramp by the fruit bowl.

Thunder rumbles the floor. Benji pulls open the silverware drawer and takes out a butcher's knife. He hands me one too—a bread knife with a serrated edge.

We move through the kitchen like rogues, his knife held high and mine held low like a staff, because this knife goes in best from underneath.

In the living room, lightning blinks over the house. Another roll of thunder, low and dangerous as I follow my brother up the stairs. The rain starts and then grows into an angry monster, beating at the roof so hard our footsteps turn silent.

Upstairs, Benji fishes his pistol out from under the mattress as I watch the door. It scares me that he has that thing, but I couldn't make him get rid of it if I tried. Dad gifted it to him before we moved away. I grab the bat from the closet in my room.

As we creep down the hallway to Mom's room, my chest suffocates with this fear of dying forever and ever. A man will jump out of the linen closet and kill me, and the back of my brother's sweater vest, flashing under the lightning, is the thing I'd see on loop as blood seeped out of my throat.

Benji bangs on the laundry-room door, and I flinch. It leaves vibration in the silence—a backdrop for his voice.

"WHO THE FUCK IS IN HERE?!"

Silence is the only thing that responds to him. The house must be empty, but it doesn't feel like it is.

"We should turn on all the lights," I whisper.

"Good idea."

He goes right and I go left, to flip switches, crank knobs, and pull strings—laundry, hallway, Mom's bathroom. Her vanity, with the jewelry stands draped in necklaces, is still full. If this were a burglar, they would have destroyed that . . .

I meet Benji at the top of the stairs. The house seems safe now, so we let out the breaths we were holding. I awkwardly laugh and let the bat loosen in my wrist.

And then, as if someone has been watching our every move from a power box, the lights all go off.

Benji and I huddle like two shadows under the all-encompassing shadow of our house. The rain beats at the roof like it's angry we exist.

"It's a ghost," I mutter.

Benji rolls his eyes. "It's not a ghost. It's a killer is what it is. Whoever killed our neighbor."

"Are you kidding or serious?"

Benji pulls out his phone, clicks on the flashlight, and raises the blinding beam right in my face. "Why would I be kidding?"

I squint against it, raise my hand.

We don't know how Matteo died. It could have very well been a sadistic serial killer on the loose in our neighborhood. I can't figure out which is scarier.

Benji calls the cops and then Mom. In the span of an hour, my house breaks out into an episode of *CSI*.

I step outside, walk over by the mailbox, and let Benji do the talking.

The cold, fresh air sticks in my throat as the fog and ecto-mist seethe around my house and Matteo's. Two ghouls are lying on the lawn, which is quiet now that the crime scene has moved to my house. They're lying side by side, their arms crossed over their chests, like a married couple in one coffin.

⁘

I came closest to the monsters when I was ten. It was in my old house's basement, which I went down to explore in the middle of the night.

A jingle emanated all the way up to my room, like the music from a jack-in-the-box.

At the bottom of the stairs, there was a ghost. I'd nicknamed him Swamp Steve because his hair was scraggly and dirty, like he'd just emerged from a swamp. He was rocking back and forth, hugging his knees, whisper-singing to himself, *"Half a pound of treaaacle. That's the way the money goes."*

I thought it was a corpse in front of him. Looked like a dug-up body. An arm was ripped off, its socket a mauve gap with dry tendons hanging out like power cords. But the thing rose, and I realized it was only a ghoul, gnawing on a piece of its own arm.

Swamp Steve sang, *"Pop goes the weasel,"* and broke into a fit of giddy laughter.

I scrambled up the stairs on my hands and feet, splintering

my knee. I was halfway to the top when a cold, hard hand gripped my ankle and yanked me backward. I spun around, kicking, and my foot went through the ghoul's face, reducing its entire skull to a plume of smoke.

Steve began singing again, louder. *"Half a pound of black en-er-gy! Half a pound of power!"*

I leapt upward two steps at a time, toward the light spilling out of the door.

"Pop go the people!"

⁙

"Jake, come inside, please!" Mom's waving me into the house because the officers are leaving now.

I walk past them with no acknowledgment. Mom says we should install security cameras on the front door, patio door, and first-floor windows.

The thing is . . . none of the doors or windows were unlocked when we got here. There were no fingerprints in the blood scrawl either. It's like someone imagined the letters into existence.

Nobody can explain the stuff ghosts do, because nobody can see it happening, So everyone is treating this like a breaking and entering and nothing else.

But it *is* something else. And I'm the only one who'll be able to take care of it, because I'm the only one who knows that it's real.

⁙

I should be sleeping, but I can't get that sloppy blood and those letters out of my head.

I'm under the comforter with my laptop, switching between a mindless conversation with Grady and research on the Heritage shooting last November. Matteo became known as a survivor, so the news thought to connect his death back to the occasion. The backlight sears my eyes as I read the chilling headlines.

SCHOOL SHOOTER OPENS FIRE ON CLASSMATES AND THEN TAKES HIS OWN LIFE

6 DEAD AND 12 WOUNDED IN DEVASTATING HERITAGE SHOOTING

AN UNTHINKABLE ACT

A SHOCKING SLAUGHTER

WHAT WAS THE MOTIVE?

Sawyer Doon's face is sprawled across every page—the same picture of him in this gray hoodie, deadpanning the camera. Average white kid, hooked nose. Would've probably grown up to wear a pinstriped shirt and some khakis and sit in a cubicle. He's not nice to look at or bad-looking. He's kind of just . . . there.

Tap-tap-tap-tap-tap-tap.

Where is that coming from?

I always hear sounds, especially when it's dark, from dead world, even when they're far away. Sound is not a physical property here. It's just everywhere, even when you don't know where it's coming from. It could be something completely harmless. A woodpecker that wood-pecked itself to death.

S.A.D. . . . the shooter from the news was named Sawyer Doon. He killed people at Matteo's school and then himself, and now S.A.D. himself could have broken into my house and left his mark on my wall. It could be the long acronym for Sawyer's name Sawyer . . . something . . . Doon.

I close my laptop, set it on my nightstand, and fall into my pillow.

There are several theories for why death loops happen. Mine

is that the people who end up trapped just didn't see it coming, so their minds got stuck in a glitch. As opposed to some people who did see it coming, because they brought it on themselves. Maybe ghosts who killed themselves get more autonomy when they cross over.

I curl up in the fetal position and try to relax.

The room is dark in all places but two—an orange salt lamp night-light and the red display on my nightstand clock, showing 2:00 a.m.

The tapping sounds like a ticking now, like a broken clock. *Tick-tick-tick-tick-tick*. Or someone with long fingernails tapping them to a desk.

Where is that coming from?

I get under the covers just to toss and turn, to be too cold and then too hot, to put the pillow over my head to mask the sound of the clock, or the timer, or whatever's responsible for that *tick-tick-tick-tick-tick-tick-tick*.

I fall asleep, my mind rationalizing the ticking as a piece of background noise.

BOOM.

I jerk up in bed and pass straight through the covers, my body like a feather floating slowly to the ceiling. My hands are framed in a crystalline blue light. My room is teeming with ecto-mist and peeling mint-green wallpaper. The walls are adorned with oval mirrors and the black-and-white photos of a family that lived here before—white people in high-waisted jackets and sequined dresses.

My light fixture has transformed into a brass ceiling fan, which spins right and then left, shaking ecto-mist like snow from its blades as it glitches in its loop of dysfunction.

I lower myself to the side of my bed, where my feet sink

beneath the creeping mist that traces the floor. The carpet is both crimson red and white, the colors shifting in tricks of light.

BOOM!

I gasp at the noise, and the dead-world air enters my throat like crushed ice.

Someone is banging on a door downstairs.

The carpet sinks around my feet like quicksand pulling me through the floor. The ecto-mist gathers under me to form a bed of clouds, which lifts me and guides me forward. In the doorway I peek back at my bed and find myself in it, fast asleep. The fluffy blue comforter stands in stark modern contrast to the the old wallpaper and the oval mirrors.

The mist pushes me away from my body, toward the ticking beyond my bedroom door.

There are tremors in the silence, in the combo of the here and the forgotten. Unintelligible whispers hiss like snakes as I glide down the second-floor hallway and an unfriendly soundscape captures the quiet.

Hssssssssssssssssss.

The mist at the top of the stairs is so thick it obscures all depth, and I don't know where I'd fall if the floor completely disappeared. There's no downstairs floor—only pieces of stairs peeking up from the shadows. I descend the stairs one at a time, but my feet don't feel a thing except the cold mist around them, and then it rises, up under my arms, through my ears.

I reach my hand out for the banister, but instead of mahogany wood I find cold iron diving toward the bottom of my house like the drop of a roller coaster.

The picture frames on the wall down the staircase seem to be floating of their own free will, exchanging themselves for older pictures. Lightning blinks over the house, and the photo-shoot set of me, mom, and Benji from five years ago fades into a photo of a little white girl in a plaid dress. She's standing in front of an old home from the 1800s. Her dad holds a hoe behind her, and her mom, a shovel.

In the foyer there's a candle chandelier that isn't my house's. The mist seethes.

The kitchen is full of things that don't belong to the house today—ugly green countertops. Moldy bread and rotten fruit. A spray of flies circles the food. Pots hang from a rack in the ceiling.

I'm losing control of my body, lifting some and then falling, like a puppet string is playing with my limbs. The window to the patio door appears like a two-way mirror on a velvet wall, an opening to the night outside.

Lightning jumps through the plastic in the slats along with weeping shadows from swaying trees.

Everything goes dark, and I'm floating in total blackness and watching the window like a lonely viewer in a movie theater at night.

There's a shadow out there. A person. A man, walking back and forth like he's nervous.

His shape is like mine—skinny, but he's hunched, like a gremlin.

He claws at the air, gathering mist in a vortex. A ring of ecto-mist forms between his hands as he moves them in a circle. This mist . . . it's not the electric-blue color I'm used to. It's red, like blood.

He walks back and forth. The wood groans underneath him as a garble escapes his mouth. *Grrblgrrblgblrrrrrrrrglbrrrrrr.* It's like something's drowning in his throat.

His movements become more abstract and odd.

He walks in tight circles. *"We're bonded now, Matteo. Inside and out. One and then another. We look out for each other."*

Hissing—intense hissing, like colonies of warring serpents. No, an army of cicadas. Chattering.

And then, a tragic weeping, like a grieving mother.

"Shut up." The voice of the person—the poltergeist—thunders from everywhere as if it's responding to the whispers. *"SHUT UP. SHUT UP, I SAID!"*

I can't rip my eyes away from his head and neck, which seems ripped through by the air itself, like a biscuit tin popped and spiraling. His skin is the color of caulk, and it's in constant motion, there in one angle and fading in the next. His hair is ratty like cornstalk. He grabs a fistful of it, and lightning blinks to reveal his pale, expressionless eyes. He's looking directly at me.

"Shut up . . ." He hits his head against the glass—BOOM. And again, like he's using it as a battering ram.

My family will be waking up. They will hear this in their world too.

Or will they? Sounds like that—loud thumps—tend to carry from dead world to the waking realm.

Any minute now someone will come and save me from this before the glass shatters . . .

Or . . . this thing is going to break in and murder me.

"Shut up . . ." His voice is like an old, rusty locomotive. "No!"

His face . . . It's the same face of the shooter on the news.

I knew it. Matteo's killer was not human.

This ghost of Sawyer Doon has skipped its death loop and decided, of its own free will, to come back and kill more people.

Now it's at my house.

"LET GO OF ME!" He's banging his head against the window, like he's punishing himself. "NEVER."

He pulls his head back by the hair, and light washes away the scene. A tug of wind snatches me through the darkness. I catapult upward through space, through the walls of my house, their boundaries immaterial now. Streaks of blue and pink spill through my eyes as ecto-mist rushes like volcanic vapor over my body. And then I'm gasping myself awake, coming from the cold opaque astral state to the box of my bedroom.

There's a blinding white beam in my face. "Jake." When Benji cuts the flashlight off, the hallway light outlines his silhouette. "You're having a nightmare."

I . . . Was I?

I lift myself out of my own sweat and plant my feet on the floor, pushing my hands into the mattress. "Oh, boy."

"Oh, boy, indeed."

"What was I saying?"

"Um . . . *shut up, let go of me, no* . . . sounded like you were fighting a kidnapper."

The ghost on the patio . . . spoke through me in my sleep?

"Anyway," Benji says. "Don't be so scared. Mom says we're getting the cameras tomorrow."

"Cameras won't do anything about the real problem."

"Ugh. Don't start talking about netherworld demons, please."

✥

He was done with it all when I was five and he was six. I interrupted his gaming to tell him there was a whole possum in our backyard.

"You're lying," he said.

"No, there really is!" I insisted. "I bet you ten dollars."

I led him to the patch of grass where I heard the creature

yowling from under the ground. He dug a hole just to prove to me there was nothing down there. What I found was a possum running in circles around the walls of its grave, and what he found was a skeleton wrapped in a dirty white T-shirt, worms and bugs clinging to the bones.

"You owe me ten dollars."

Benji reburied the corpse with his foot and didn't talk to me for three weeks.

⁂

He trudges out of my room now and clicks off the hallway light before I can respond. I follow and approach the top of the stairs as his bedroom door clicks shut behind me.

A roll of thunder shakes the foundation of the house as I put my foot on stair one. My hand squeezes the polished wood of the bannister, grateful to have something sturdy in it. From here I can see the entryway and the living room, but the patio door off the kitchen is hidden.

I move down the stairs and through the kitchen. The blinds are shut. There was someone out there when I was asleep, but it could have been a nightmare. Sometimes I can't tell the ghosts in my mind from the real thing.

The house rumbles as I reach for the door to the patio. In the kitchen, a time flashes green on the oven display: 2:06 a.m. The power was out, and I didn't even realize it. I'm not all there, I guess—not fully awake.

Through the blinds, the platform outside is empty. Nothing but the pots where Mom's plants have died.

No people, and no ghosts.

SAWYER

October 17

Dear Diary,

It's so easy these days to doze off in the sopped leaves. I know I'm only seventeen, but I'm ready to move out. Somewhere dank and dark. Maybe a tree house. It stormed out here last night, and I ventured out, found the spot where the most rain crashed through the canopy, and lay in the mud until I became a part of the melting earth.

I love the smell of wood and rain.

Some nights I sleep in the shed. On days when I have to see my doctor, a spear of sunlight wakes me up as Momma cracks the door open.

"Sawyer! Sawyer Adalwolf!" she screams on repeat. It's no wonder I hate the sound of my name.

I always have to talk to someone. It's not a six-foot-tall Italian man anymore, but an old man who wears grandpa sweaters and falls asleep on me.

His name is Dr. Scott. Dr. Scott has said I suffer from severe clinical depression, and it "may be something else," but he "has to see."

Our first exercise was journaling, hence me writing these.

The car ride to the office was silent today because Momma doesn't talk to me about it much—she talks to him about it.

To me, she says, "I'll be back to get you in an hour," as I dump myself out of the car and enter the Hapeville Hospital lobby, where everyone is sullen, ashamed, or petrified. Sick people and their stressed relatives eat food-court food and contemplate their mortality.

I take the elevator to the sixth floor, where Dr. Scott greets me with a forced grin. We sit across from each other, like opponents, him in the chair, me on the unsupportive couch cushions. The silence is patronizing.

"Sawyer." The doctor purses his lips and checks that his silver-blond hair is pushed behind his ears every time we talk.

There are minutes of silence, with just my name hanging in the air, with the white noise of his sound machine. "I need you to work with me if you want to get better," he says.

It's bittersweet—the connection between his paycheck and my wellness. He really doesn't care that I am better, but I have to seem better.

Today, he leaned out of his chair and tossed a pen and pad on the couch next to me, like he was prompting a dog with a bone. I was supposed to write my goals for the school year or something.

If I could've been honest, I'd have told him, "My one hope for the school year is that everyone else survives." He'd have found it alarming, so I didn't write anything down.

"I think you should try talking to someone new when you're finally ready to go back to school." His suggestions were so very simple. "Make a new friend. Just start with a hello."

"I don't want to make new friends."

"Why not?"

"People don't like me."

"Why do you say that?"

"It's true."

"Okay," he said. "No friends, then. What do you want to do this year that's challenging, or exciting, or would motivate you?"

"Nothing."

"Do you enjoy school?"

"Not at all."

"Nothing you enjoy? No favorite subject?"

Dissecting frogs in biology was fun for me. That's it.

Dr. Scott got real transfixed by those swirly metal things on top of the roof next door. When we were out of time, he could barely conceal his excitement to move on to a more interesting, open patient. Even the guy paid to care about me doesn't really care.

"Is there anything else you wanted to talk about today?" Dr. Scott asked at the end of our session.

I wanted to talk about why he's never been able to give me a better answer to why my brain works so differently from the people around me. I think that this is a cause for alarm. Dr. Scott, however, yawns in our appointments. As casual as if everything is under control.

On any given night I don't know whether I'll hurt someone else or myself, and I dream of ways to do it, to inflict pain and test the body's limits. I don't know why it fascinates me. I should be in a ward, but the doctor won't stop patronizing me enough to admit I'm beyond repair. He stares out of the window in my silence, but I never look away from him. I pictured his head in a bread bag today for no reason.

❖

Everything was quiet on the ride home. I was deciding how much I'd share with Dr. Scott when the right time came. Bill thought medication interrupted the natural flow of the body, so I never got help when I really needed it.

Every week growing up, Bill slapped me around with his hand or an empty beer bottle and told me to "gimme your best shot." I first hit him back when I was fifteen, and he punched me so hard a tooth fell out.

"Oh, Lord!" Momma ran over with a wet paper towel and pressed it to my lip.

"That's what makes a man!" Bill roared.

Both my parents were laughing.

That was the same year Bill went on a business trip for some cable-selling convention and Momma said he wouldn't be home for a long time. I didn't know then that meant never, but considering how much I'd begun to hate him, it's probably a good thing he never came back.

JAKE

Monday morning, I sit next to Fiona in English, drop the bag at my feet, and take out *The Great Gatsby*. Ms. Kingston arrives and wishes us an exhausted good morning as she slogs to the class computer.

"Attendance . . . ," she groans.

She goes down the list of names. I haven't done the reading again, so I open the book to sneak in a skim, maybe catch some key words that will help me survive the discussion. But . . . in running my fingers absently through the pages, I notice they feel weird.

"Anna," Ms. Kingston says, followed by a responding *Here!* "Paul."

"Here."

The pages are brittle and drawn over. A big red **6** is blocking the introduction. It's too thick and heavy to be permanent marker, and it's making the whole page crinkle around it. On the next page is another **6**, then on each page after that a different character: **7. R. E. D.** Big letters, like a message, on every . . . single . . . page. And they're drawn in dried blood.

"What the hell is that?" says Chad Roberts, not minding his own business. He's two chairs down from me today, electing not to be right across from me, but closer. He's leaning over Fiona to gawk at my book. "That how you mark up all your books, Livingston?" His tone is as shaky as I am. "In ritual blood sacrifice?"

Why are you so obsessed with me?

There's some laughter, some recognition that something weird is going on with me. Everyone is pulling out their books. People poke their heads out to look at the strange symbols—the message drawn in blood. I can smell it. Like burning wood and iron.

Can they?

"What's going on?" Ms. Kingston approaches me, hand hanging coyly over the belt at her pencil skirt, neck like a curious vulture. "Jake?" Her mouth widens in horror as her boots boom against the floor. "What have you done?"

My hand won't stop holding the page open. It's frozen by fear, or shame, maybe. I didn't do this, but it feels like I did, because who else could've? I'm trapped between this impulse to hide it and to ask for help. But of course, no one can help me.

"Sorry . . ." I flip pages frantically. Seems like the whole book is destroyed. "I didn't do this."

It feels like the person who did this is in the room with me, laughing at the misery of my embarrassment. *"Ha ha ha ha ha ha!"*

Can they hear that?

No, everyone is straight-faced, all judgmental stares. And that chorus of children laughing is coming from dead world, maybe even the classroom next door, where someone laughed so much they curled up and died.

I don't want to be here anymore.

I close my book and push out from the table. The chair legs groan, and Ms. Kingston flinches. With my bag, I launch from the room like an escape capsule and dart to the end of the hallway.

The running feels good, like if my stride is long enough, it will rip my blazer and slacks and everything will fall off of me. I'll crash through the window like a half-naked superhero and fly into the sun.

Head swimming, I shuffle down the stairwell and collapse on the landing, letting my bag fall off one arm.

6 6 7 R E D R U T H R O A D. 667 Redruth Road. An address down the street from mine. Matteo's? Yes . . . it must be Matteo's.

It's a book with letters written in blood. The same blood from my walls.

I'm being led to him with a blood trail. But why?

Footsteps approach down the stairs above me, and Fiona appears on the landing with her bag, like she has no intention of returning to class. She sits next to me, swinging her backpack onto her lap.

"Hi," I say.

"Hey!" Her face is heart-shaped and dimpled, her eyes magnified behind a pair of round glasses. Her hair falls in two pigtails over either shoulder, resting on the lapels of her blazer. She crosses her legs so the plaid skirt forms a blanket at her knees and pulls out a box of crackers. "Seaweed nougat?"

"What's that?"

"Delicious."

I eat a cracker. It's savory with a sweet filling. "That is good. Did Ms. Kingston send you out?"

"I walked out."

"Why?"

"Because . . . I really feel like they're ganging up on you." She chews and speaks with her mouth half-full. "Chad and Ms. Kingston. Chad probably did that to your book. Seems like a stunt he'd pull."

"You think?"

"He stares at you a lot. I've noticed that." She pulls her knees to her chest and rests her hands on her saddle shoes. And then she faces down the stairs, where a teacher's footsteps are clacking in the hallway.

We jump to our feet at the same time, then rush up the stairs and out of sight. She's laughing like we got away with something. "Do you ever hate it here?" she asks.

"Every day."

She spins around the landing like a ballerina dulled in the light. "Do you want to have lunch together today?"

"Yeah, of course!"

Her eyebrows rise at my enthusiasm, and I'm a little embarrassed—I don't usually get so excited. But then, nobody's ever invited me to lunch except for Grady, and Jalen from my old school, who I never see anymore and will probably never see again.

⁘

The fountains and tables in the lunch courtyard are like what you'd find in the garden of an elusive aristocrat from the dark ages. Statues of cherubs holding cornucopias of fruit. In the middle of the courtyard, a stone version of Sam the saber cat—our mascot, pisses water from his mouth and into a pool of pennies.

We take a table in the nook of a brick wall and a hedge. Fiona unzips a lunch bag and stares at my hand.

Ecto-mist has been thicker in the air all day, erupting in quick lightning strikes, centralizing in pockets of static storm clouds. That's probably why there are zigzags and bubbles scribbled across my knuckles. Sometimes that world consumes my every thought. Sometimes all I hear is screaming—like now.

Someone is screaming, and it sounds like there's water in their throat. Fiona's mouth is moving, but I can't even hear the words.

"What's wrong?" she asks.

I flinch, snapping back to reality.

"*AAAAHHHHHHHHHHH!*" I wonder where that's coming from.

The rugby boys are tossing a ball around people eating their lunch. They've come out of their blazers and are now just in their button downs, some with the buttons undone to reveal the muscle at the top of their chests and the little chains with the silver crosses that so many of them seem to wear.

"Jake?"

"Sorry."

People call my name all the time—I think more than I even notice. I try my best every day to be better about paying attention.

Fiona holds out a bag of chips to me, and I invite myself to two or three. I don't like Doritos, but I like being offered things, because it makes me feel welcome, in a way. I can't remember the last time I had lunch at school with anyone other than Grady. But he's in tutoring today, and I'm grateful for that.

She looks at the graying red meat on my tray. "What kind of meat is that?"

"I think it's a rabbit?"

"You don't know?" She smiles, and there's a fang in her gums.

St. Clair kids have a thing for game meat. Things you'd hunt in the woods—deer, goat, roebuck, moose. You might catch those kids in hunting hats on social media posing with cadavers, which is why I'm afraid of social media—people that I don't even talk to started to send me friend requests, and I didn't want them, but it would've been rude to deny them. So I deleted all of my accounts instead, and now I live off the map.

I haven't had much to eat in four days beyond bites of sandwiches. Benji and I installed three security cameras on Saturday. Figures have been zooming by when I enter and leave rooms, but they're never there when I stop to look at them. The sky has been so dreary, so full of death, like a cold blanket, and I'm almost certain I'm sinking slowly upward into it.

A bomb lands on the corner of my tray, flipping off the meat and potatoes.

Not a bomb, a soccer ball. Rolling on the ground by our table.

"Incoming!" Chad's warning comes a little too late. He flings his body over me to retrieve the ball.

"Can y'all be more careful?" Fiona barks.

"My bad, li'l Chan."

I run my fingers along my tie and lapel buttons to check for any splatter.

Chad tucks the ball under his big arm and turns his lipless mouth into a baby pout. "Sorry about your little lunchy-lunch, Jake."

And he waltzes away.

Fiona watches me. "I'm sorry, Jake. That guy's such an asshole. I hope somebody kicks his ass someday. Gives him a taste of his own medicine." She's small but sturdy, with thick forearms. She'd probably beat Chad in a fight sooner than I could.

I hate myself for being such a pushover.

I'm tired of losing these spats and sitting with quiet resentment. Fiona is right. Chad is one of the few people I wouldn't miss if some happenstance misfortune cut his life short.

SAWYER

October 21

Dear Diary,

Dr. Scott and Momma can't agree on what's wrong with me. Doc says, "I don't want to assume the worst. Sawyer's a good kid."

I think he's lying to make everybody feel better. He asks me pretty often what would make me happy. I think seeing someone evil like Matteo Mooney in extreme pain would bring me to what others call "joy." Doc Scott harps on about serotonin like it's the secret to life.

Momma asks him what's wrong with me, and he says, "He just has trouble relating."

I went back to school today, nineteen days after discharge. Too soon, I think, but I had no choice.

Word about my suicide attempt spread while I was gone. I can tell by how people look at me—and I blame it on my big-mouthed sister, whose friends are popular and ensure everyone knows everything about everybody.

People mostly stay out of your way when they think you're crazy. Everyone stared at me, but they left me alone. In every classroom I was fragile glass. A bomb that could go off at any moment.

But people like Matteo—popular kids—don't give a shit how sad you are. Actually, they want you to be sadder. Annie is kind of friends with him—she tends to leech on to whoever's getting the most attention.

Today we were in the bathroom at the same time. I caught him in an awkward moment where we looked at each other and instantly looked away. I went into the stall, and he banged on the door after I shut it. "Little Sawyer!" He put one unfeeling gray eye in the crack of the hinge and watched me. "Why'd you try to hurt yourself, little Sawyer?"

I pressed myself against the wall. And he laughed and moved on.

I'm glad my bigmouthed sister let everyone know I am fragile.

Sophomore year, when I ran cross-country, the bullying was nonstop. He thrashed me with towels; he pulled down my pants; he hid my shoes somewhere and left me to search the locker room for them as everyone left. I finally found them wedged in the cavity of a toilet when the whole place was abandoned. Matteo was blocking the doorway, stretching his big arms across the passage. He had no shoes on, only socks, spikes hanging by the laces from his fingers.

"Found your shoes?" His scowl was made of hatred that day.

I tried to sneak under his arm, and he grabbed me by the shirt. "Uh-uh. Not so fast." Threw me in a stall. Struck me with the bottom of his spikes.

"Stop fucking looking at me all the time." There was murder in his voice.

Bright blood trickled down my arm, got stuck to the hairs. I sucked spit through my teeth as he pulled me off the toilet and threw me into a urinal. I caught myself on the flush valve.

"Hey." He twisted me to face him, punched me in the ribs. "Fight back. Why won't you fight me back, you pussy?"

I didn't answer. I only wished a flying sword could fall from the sky and impale his beautiful head.

I admire his beauty. His olive skin, powerful arms, the smell of Axe, seductive and suffocating. Rock-hard pecs, hair gelled and dark like a greaser from the fifties. He's so beautiful and violent.

My one friend sophomore year was Kieran Waters—kid came from Nebraska or somewhere to Heritage, so he was just lost everywhere he looked. We sat next to each other in class and talked a bit, but after the first few weeks, he started to look at me sideways and frown, and I knew it was coming—that moment where he'd leave me like they all do.

He pulled me into a stairwell after gym class one day. "Sawyer, you gotta start talking more," he said. "You ignore half the stuff I say. You barely respond to what anybody says. And you sit there and smile all big to yourself all the time and pull your hair out. Why do you do that? It's so weird. Also . . . sorry to ask, but are you gay?"

I had no answer for that because it wasn't my problem what people thought.

I'm put off by humans in general. I admire them so much in appearance. Kieran's hair . . . I liked it because it was like a kamikaze, like a huge, all-destroying firebomb. His Adam's apple was softball-sized, his limbs like bowstrings you could pluck and make music with. His bones were so visible.

I watched him. Maybe he thought I was gay because of how I watched him.

"Are you gay, Sawyer?" He jabbed me in the shoulder. "Huh? Are you? Answer me!"

I blinked and studied the protrusion of his collarbones, like two marbles baked beneath a crust. Everyone has always felt so hostile toward the fact that I enjoy the male form.

Kieran stormed away when I didn't answer. I smiled to myself as he left. He was so angry.

I guess I'm so quiet because I'm under no obligation to speak, and people choose to let that bother them.

Today, on my first day back, we passed each other in the hallway. He'd trimmed his hair down to short spiked waves, probably to fit in. He looked so guilty when he saw me. I felt kind of bad for him, but then I didn't.

Kieran is still gorgeous, even without the hair. Beautiful and fragile like a porcelain tea set. It seems impossible to turn something so pretty so ugly, but it's not. Everything turns ugly after it's dead.

JAKE

An avenue is all that separates Matteo's house from mine. Our houses are like faces in a staring match, and all the other houses form parallel columns from here to there, like watchers on the sidelines, waiting for a showdown.

It's 6:55 and dark for the day. October is sleepy and sad, and I'm in the swivel chair by my window, just observing. That house is blue, with two stories and a garage. Rectangular windows on the bottom floor, square on floor two, and a circle at the top.

I drew a picture of the house, but the angles were ugly. I balled it up and tossed it. The current sketch in my lap is of Sawyer Doon—long hair, distant eyes, lips barely lips. More like receding lines.

How could you?

A black Mercedes cuts its headlights around the corner at the end of the street and parks at Matteo's house. I throw the sketchpad aside and poke my binoculars through the blinds, catching gray-haired Mr. Mooney in the scope, bunched between the seat and wheel. The car goes still, and he sits there, sad bags like worm sacks under his eyes. The aura of grief leaks like waste gas from his ears, filling the car with an indigo smog.

He opens the door, swings out a leg. His business slacks are choking his thigh to death. There's a ghoul by his mailbox, tilting its head at him, but in the binoculars, it looks like a vanishing shape in the fog. Mr. Mooney and his ghoul . . . they're mirroring each other. Caught in this moment of *What's it gonna be? Life or death?*

The dad stands up, twitchy and forced. The ghoul stands too, tall as the house, casting its shadow in the man's wake. He walks inside. The ghoul watches, like a silent titan, an omen of bad things to come.

I slide back from the window and light the wilderness incense on my book cart, pick up my rose quartz ring, and slide it over my finger.

If only I could wear this gorgeous pink stone in public. It's soft and protective. But someone would laugh at me.

I pour eucalyptus oil into my diffuser and pull my ceramic elephant to my chest.

There's something molding in my gut. Death wants something to do with this place, and it's dazing. Ghosts, ghouls, and ecto-mist were never meant to be so important, but suddenly they've decided to weave their way into my immediate surroundings, too close for comfort.

Sawyer's face looks at me from the sketchpad. I may have made the eyes so dark they're all-seeing and catch you wherever you are. I'm only good at drawing the bad things.

⁌⁍

Grady tries to get me interested in a band later that night over Messenger.

GRADY: DUDE. Listen to Pushing Crazies—
"Death on a Lollipop." Mindblowing.

ME: Will do when I get a chance.

GRADY: You probably won't like it.
It's not sad alt-r&b.

ME: that's not all i listen to

GRADY: Sure. Whatever you say.

There's a knock at my door, and Mom's already entering before I say come in. When she was a flight attendant, she spent all day and night smiling at travelers and telling them, "Welcome!" Now she's a pilot, so she wears a different uniform with a white shirt and navy tie. She traded in the skirt for pants but kept the thick bottom heels and dangling amethyst earrings. When she has no planes to fly, when she's here with me and Benji for the night, she's found in a black bonnet and silk nightgown, pecan-brown skin shiny and free of makeup.

She sits at the end of the bed. "You good?"

I give her a lackluster nod. I'm not good, but I never am, really. Only pretending.

"Have you added any new schools to your list?"

I shake my head. "Just Augusta, Kennesaw State, Georgia Southern, and SCAD."

"You don't think you'll need more? You should start with at least ten. You want your reach schools, your likely schools, and your safety schools."

Once again, she looks worried about my lack of engagement. She knows I've never been much of an A student. B+ at best. But it's hard for me sometimes to waste time wondering where I'll go once I leave home, when I can barely figure out how to manage my day-to-day life.

"I'm still looking," I assure her.

"Alright. Don't forget I'm going to Jamaica this weekend."

I'm not happy for the reminder. She only flies for about half the month, but when she's gone it's for days at a time, and sometimes a full week. Most kids would be excited about that. It just makes me feel alone.

"I'm counting on you to hold things down," she says. "Make sure the dishes get done and your brother doesn't leave his underwear on the floor."

I can't be an older brother to my older brother.

"I'll try," I say, but what I really mean is *I can't control anything Benji does. I wish I didn't have to think about it.*

My mom is my only good parent, but I still feel muted around her, like I'm not the person she's hoping I am and if I say too much, my cover will be blown. Mostly I feel empty and lost on questions like "You good?" I have no reference point to know what good or bad is. I'm only existing. I guess that means I'm good.

"Thank you for being responsible, Jake." She kisses me on the forehead and leaves the room.

I look at the house down the street, through the half-open blinds. The lights are off in the upper windows.

I think there's something there I'm meant to see.

✧

I used to wake up unable to move. Asleep and awake at the same time. Aware and not. I would see figures standing in the corner of my bedroom. Giant shadows with no eyes, pressing themselves up against the wall.

Tonight, when I wake up, it's to a silent room full of waste. A glass lampshade on an old nightstand colored like dragonfly wings. There's a wardrobe, a horseshoe above the door. An overflow of old desks with attached mirrors, their frames tucked with tickets to the opera. Golf clubs and tennis rackets floating, and water drooling from the plaster in the corner.

The mist comes down from the ceiling in wires, which fasten around my soul and lift it. My soul pulls from my body and floats to the window. Behind me, my physical self remains curled up, hands under the pillow, like an angel.

I'm moving away from myself.

Goodbye, I whisper to my body. I've never felt married to it. Astral projecting sometimes feels more natural, because I don't have to do anything—the mist steers my journeys for me.

The window glass approaches me, and behind the blinds is Redruth Road, the houses of my avenue, their white paint and blue roofs. I drift through the plaster of my house, a deep coldness densifying in my throat. The bricks pull me apart as I go through them, and then I'm pieced back together. The sky is a deep space of garnet and black casting hellish shade over the houses.

And the houses are in chaos. Chimneys erode in their own smoke; fences crumble like castle gates under siege. A house burns in eternal flame. A man—someone's dad, or a roofer—trips and rolls backward off a roof, landing on his head and bursting into light.

I'm like an astronaut drifting through a dangerous galaxy cluster. At the end of the street is a devastated planet.

A gunshot pops the silence, and with it, the bulb of a streetlamp pops. It rebuilds itself while the sparkling asphalt twenty feet below turns into Matteo's driveway. I'm floating over his fence, through the glass of his windows, which cut me open like an arctic wind.

This house was custom built. There's nothing old about

the room. The beanbags, trophy shelf, and workout bench all belonged to him. Music plays from the cracked door in the connecting bathroom, where a sliver of light spills out. Then I'm sinking through his bathroom door just in time for Matteo Mooney to step onto his bath mat, snag a towel from the rack, and fold it around his waist.

He greets himself in the mirror, pushes wet brown hair to one side, dabs his stubble with shaving cream.

In this mirror I'm invisible as a ghost. I might as well be a ghost. All I see in place of myself is the natural stone of his shower—a cut above the tile in mine.

Matteo sprays Axe all over himself as something sneaks into the corner of the mirror.

It's a knife. A butcher's knife, poking through the crack of the door and angled down, like someone's holding it, ready to stab. Matteo comes out of the trance of his music. He sees it. Freezes. Widens his eyes and—

"Fuck!" He nicks himself with the razor and falls into the towel rack. "What the fuck?!"

The knife speeds toward his chest. Matteo dives for the bathtub, catching on the shower curtain. A ring goes *snap!*, and he folds, legs tumbling over the side.

The knife hits the wall, pulls away, does a flip through the air.

"Whoa, whoa, whoa, *wait!*" Matteo holds his hands up in surrender, like he can reason with the knife. "Stop!"

It can't hear him . . . or whatever ghost is holding it isn't listening.

The weapon traces an *S* in the air over his body. Matteo stands up in the tub so he's face-to-face with it.

Run! I think, and the word rattles like an echo from the end of a cave. *"Run!"*

It's too late. The knife has come to the end of its acronym. **S.A.D.** The same letters slathered all over the wall of my house. The same thing that wrote them is the thing that killed Matteo. It's the thing that was on my patio and the face that was on the news. The menace that has come to my neighborhood.

Sawyer Doon.

The knife impales Matteo's abs, turning his muscle to soft stomach. It yanks itself out and goes in again harder.

"St-stop . . ." His voice is weak as he slides down the wall, eyes fading, blood seeping over his belly button.

The blade poises for another stab as the astral wind tugs me through space, sending me in backward flight through Matteo's bedroom, through his walls, and back outside.

I've seen what I needed to see.

The street rewinds beneath me as the house I've just left shrinks. Through the window, I watch as Matteo crawls from the bathroom, a geyser of blood gushing down his chin.

Help, he mouths, and his head hits the floor.

It's the first piece to chip away. And then the stars eat the rest of him, reducing his body to nothing.

JAKE

I spend study period with Grady in the library on Friday. He's
very distracting, but that's what I need.

Three days have passed, and I haven't been able to digest
anything. The dread in me has tampered with the pipes of my
digestive tract. Even chicken tenders don't make it past without
turning into nausea or diarrhea. And Matteo . . . poor Matteo.
I see bloody shower water leaking down the walls of my eyes
when I close them.

Grady keeps tapping my shoulder and whispering. "Did you
get a chance to listen to that band I sent you?"

"The . . . um . . . Pushing Daisies?"

"Pushing *Crazies*, bro."

Right. Pushing Crazies. "I don't think it's really my style."

"Are you kidding me, bro? First you trash Junkman's Mistress,
and now you're telling me you *didn't* like Pushing Crazies?"

"Yup. Sounds about right. Guilty."

There are bigger things at stake. I might have to burn *The
Great Gatsby* just to forget someone murderous is close enough
to me to be tampering with my books. Someone who could be
leading me on a deadly murder trail.

I'm turning back to the math problem, when I accidentally lock eyes with Fiona, who's with her friend Amanda in front of the big windows across the room. She looks just as bored as me, and honestly, I don't know why we don't just hang out together.

Grady glances at me and then back to his laptop screen, where he's typing away. "What's going on with you and Fiona?"

"What do you mean?"

"I mean, y'all keep looking at each other."

"We do?"

Making new friends is awkward as heck. Telling your old friends you want new friends? Even more awkward. I wonder if Fiona is also caught in this dilemma.

Grady sighs. "Anyway, heard your brother's throwing a Halloween thing at your place tonight, is that true?"

"If it is, I haven't been informed."

But totally makes sense, seeing as Mom left for Jamaica this afternoon. I'm disappointed but not surprised that Benji would host a wild party in her absence. It wouldn't be the first time. Guess I failed at being Benji's older brother again.

"Yeah, but it's for, like, basketball players and athletes and stoners, you know?" he says. "Cool people. I didn't get an invitation, but I was hoping since you're his brother . . ."

"I mean, if it's a bunch of popular kids getting trashed at my house, I probably won't know anybody but you."

"That's a yes, right?" He smiles giddily. "You can get me in?"

"It's not the Met Gala, Grady—it's a house party at my house."

"So we're getting trashed tonight?"

"I don't drink."

Grady rolls his eyes and then waves Fiona and Amanda over to our table. To my surprise, they actually walk up to us.

When they arrive, Amanda sits first. "Any reason you guys

were staring at us?" Amanda has pale skin, dark hair that frames her cheeks in a gothic way, and a permanently serious expression.

"I . . . wasn't staring," I say.

Fiona takes the other seat, and Grady clasps his hands on the table like a dealer at a gambling table. "Let me just be upfront with you ladies. We're just two single guys going to Jake's brother's party tonight."

Oh, brother . . .

Fiona's souring her lips and barely trying to disguise it. "Um . . . I didn't know there was a party happening."

Grady leans in. "We're not telling everybody. It's just a handful of people, you know?"

Amanda blinks her long lashes as she looks from Grady to Fiona. "A handful of *people*? I don't know what that means, but we hate parties."

"I don't hate parties." Fiona rolls her eyes like she literally doesn't know her.

"You said you hated parties," Amanda says. "We talked about this."

"I don't remember saying that?"

She grabs Fiona's wrist. "You *definitely* said that. We went to the rugby game, and you specifically said you didn't want to go to the after-party. I remember because I had to return my dress."

Fiona pulls her arm free. "That was *that* party. I didn't want to be around drunk rugby boys. That doesn't mean I hate parties in general."

"So, like, *what's* the difference?" I swear it's like Amanda's eyeballs will boing out their sockets.

"I get why you wouldn't want to come to the hood," I say, making her notice me finally.

She grimaces in my direction. "The . . . *hood*?"

"Clark City. Well, it's hood-adjacent. Not fully gentrified yet."
Her eyes are petrified circles. "Why would we have a party there?"

Amanda is from Sunwood, named for its prestigious private university, known for its supermalls and ice cream stores that sell pumpkin-spice flavor. To her, *hood* and *hood-adjacent* are the same thing.

"I'll see what I'm doing later on," Fiona says.

Amanda's mouth opens with offense. She rips her purse off the back of the chair and stands up. "I'll see you after school." She stomps across the floor to the stairs, arms hugging a stack of books.

The air ripples in Amanda's wake, conjuring a ghost who's coming toward us.

I buck back in my chair but not enough for anyone to notice.

It's the shooter from the picture on the news. Sawyer. Blond hair sweeping like greasy hay in front of his arctic eyes. A dark gray hoodie with a damp hole in one shoulder. Poorly fitted faded jeans.

It can't be . . .

Grady and Fiona are speaking, but their voices sound underwater. *"What's her problem?" "She has a lot of them."*

The Heritage killer is in my library in full daylight . . . walking. Free. Moving outside of his loop.

Is this real?

My hands are shaking and opaque against the book in front of me. *I am real.*

Sawyer's looking right at me, eyes focused and lifeless.

Algebra equations swim across the light, blending with each other.

You know where I live? You know where I go to school?

Sawyer's standing right behind Amanda's empty chair.

I jump back from the table and fall over, my book bag falling with me.

"Jake?" Grady says.

Sawyer lifts his arm to reveal an AR-15 jutting from his hoodie like a robotic extension. But he doesn't raise it further. He starts to sink. Into the floor. It sucks him down like quicksand.

I rise over the table to watch him go. He's calm, indifferent, like he means for it to happen, or doesn't care that the floor is digesting him. His eyes look up at me, smiling before they submerge.

Then he's gone.

A hand lands on me, and I flinch.

Fiona pulls back, arched brows pressing down with concern. "Are you okay?"

No. Never.

The bell rings—the glockenspiel shakes up activity on the study floor, reverberating through the stems and nerves of my spine.

"Fine. Gotta go. Test today." There is no test, but I have to feign normalcy.

I grab my book bag and run off in a hurry, no idea where I'm going, until finally I'm in a bathroom stall, closed inside, sitting with my feet on the toilet.

I have to breathe. To be alone and process this. I'm being followed by a menace. He knows where I live and where I go to school.

He is a school shooter.

And I may, for whatever reason, be his next victim.

⁙

"Are you sure you're okay?" Grady finds me at the end of the day when I'm on my way outside.

"Yeah, I'm fine. Think I ate something bad at lunch."

He follows me out of the school and then grabs my shoulders to steer me away from the yard and down the wide stone steps to the rugby field.

"Where are we going?"

"Trust me," he says.

We end up under the bleachers. Grady's looking around like he's about to do a drug deal.

"I don't want any crack," I announce.

"It's not crack." He pulls a silver flask from inside his jacket. "Just a little something to get you started. We gotta get you doing cool stuff, Jake. You're too timid. This is the perfect pregame recipe."

I'm on the fence on whether or not I even want to hold that while on school grounds. "What is it?"

"Just a little Tennessee whiskey. Take it, bro. You need it. You're so uptight."

I hesitate. Alcohol? Me? It's never been a thing. Why would it be?

Then again, I don't want to be an Amanda, throwing a fit just because Fiona wanted to go to a party. I don't want to be all prudish. I've never tried alcohol, but maybe it's time. Maybe it'll take the edge off the dread that's been in my stomach.

I accept the flask and drop it in my hoodie's kangaroo pocket. Grady smiles.

"That's what I'm talking about," he says. "See you tonight."

✢

I'm not sure I should be seeing anyone. My mind seems even more off than usual.

I spend most of the late afternoon sketching things. I've been drawing obsessively lately. Triangles and lightning mostly—puzzles of clouds, fire, and chaos rather than characters.

Sawyer followed me to school. The thought keeps running through my mind, blossoming more dire thoughts. *Sawyer could kill everybody. Amanda, Fiona, Grady, Benji . . . everybody.*

The flask Grady gave me watches me from my nightstand like something that's not supposed to be here. Something I have to get rid of before it gets rid of me.

I've been practically shaking ever since what I saw at Redruth Road, and now I can't even go to school in peace. This ghost killed Matteo Mooney. And I could be next.

But why? What do you want?

I toss my notebook and pencil aside. The flask ends up in my hand; I screw off the top and chug. I keep chugging even as the warm, toxic liquid burns my chest.

Gross, gross, gross.

The prospect of Sawyer murdering me in the middle of the night seems much more likely than him doing it in daylight. There would be fewer witnesses to run in, flip on lights, and gather around me to extinguish my panic.

So maybe my first answer is catching some Z's before the sun has set completely.

I curl up on the bed, hug the flask like a baby's bottle, and pour the contents into my mouth.

And pour it.

And pour it.

And . . .

SAWYER

October 26

Dear Diary,

All I do is lie in the bed in the shape of a waning moon, wondering when my house will stop feeling like a prison. The one broken panel from my ceiling fan watches me from the crack in my closet, reminding me of the ruckus I caused.

It whispers, "Ha ha, you lost."

After it broke, Annie came rushing to my room and called the ambulance. I lost consciousness from the stress the extension cord had caused to my throat.

"Hold on, Sawyer!" she cried as my eyes closed. "Hold on!"

When we cross paths in the house, she watches me like I may vanish right in front of her, and she always needs to keep track. I was walking to the kitchen earlier. She was by the front door, staring in the mirror, adding touches to her Halloween makeup for some party. Momma was in the living room in between, her eyes glued to a dating show. I took a pack of Dots from the Halloween bowl on the counter.

"Stop reading my diary, Sawyer." Annie's disembodied voice hurtled from the other room.

"I didn't read your diary," I said. "I don't read your diary."

"You think I'm stupid? I notice when you put it back wrong on the shelf."

It was very odd she'd think I'd want her innermost thoughts. I'd certainly choose to invade the thoughts of someone more talented and ambitious. "I don't care about your stupid life the way you're obsessed with mine."

"Please." She laughed. "People are only obsessed with you because you force them to be with your impulsive ways."

"Annie . . ." Momma chimed in with a warning tone as she watched the TV. "Don't start, please. Just get along."

It was probably Momma who read her diary. Momma loves to know everything about us. She snoops in our rooms and swears she doesn't. She found a stash of gay porn magazines under my bed and didn't look at me for a week.

She doesn't say sorry for anything when she knows someone is being blamed for something she did.

Annie asked a million and one questions. "Are you in there getting candy? Aren't you too old for that now? Don't you want to go to a party?"

"I don't need parties, or friends." I'll never be the people who travel in packs. She can taunt me all she wants and treat me like a problem. I'll never be those people.

"And I guess you don't want a girlfriend either?"

I stormed back to my room and slammed the door so hard the piece of shitty wood bounced right back open and I had to slam it again. I love the sound of a good slam.

Momma started screaming, "Annie, REALLY?"

She forgets that just two months ago, I almost died.

Annie came knocking on the door like clockwork. She always does the wrong thing and realizes after. But unlike Momma, she tries to apologize even though she never says the words "I'm sorry."

"Open the door, Sawyer. You have to leave the door open now, remember? Like the doctor said."

She knows everything that the doctor said except for the part about being nice to me. Telling people at school about my suicide attempt isn't nice. Neither is criticizing me.

So I didn't respond because she didn't deserve it.

"Sawyer, PLEASE," she begged. "Just open up. Can't go hurting yourself over a dumb argument. Can't handle your problems that way."

But I can. "Sawyer?"

Quiet now. Hush, and panic.

A wink spasmed at the corner of my mouth. This was fun.

"Sawyer?" Annie called.

I like to hear her weak and afraid she'd be the one to push me to my limit. It makes the pain go away. To imagine her explaining HER behavior in the aftermath of my untimely death.

"Sawyer?" The quiver in her voice was music to my ears. "Sawyer?"

Say my name. Say my name forever.

JAKE

GRADY: JAKE!!!
GRADY: BRO, WHERE ARE YOU?
GRADY: Your bro's not letting me in.
Says I'm not on the list.
GRADY: Ugh! WTF?
GRADY: ARE YOU SLEEPING????
GRADY: ARE YOU HAVING SEX WITH
FIONA???

Text messages. Way too many texts from Grady when I roll awake. I wish Grady wasn't so clingy. He should just wait for me to respond to one message before sending six more.

It's Saturday, right? Yes, it must be.

I drop my phone, squeeze my eyes shut, stumble off the mattress, and close the blinds. I have a headache, and that light is making it worse.

I zone out even when I sleep. I wake up and choose to fall back asleep, sometimes for fourteen hours at a time. My body feels so heavy in the bed.

I stumble up and out the door. There's an abandoned gold stiletto sitting all by itself in the hallway. The crime scene of last night's party is everywhere the deeper I travel through the house and down the stairs—red plastic cups, greasy napkins, orange and black glitter, Silly String stuck to the plaster.

It's coming back to me . . .

Last night, I woke up in astral form. Two ghost boys were making out against the mahogany wardrobe of my dead bedroom. They were dressed in crop tops, disco pants, and vibrant shoes. One was Black, with a Jheri curl, and one white, with flat hair and a headband. They undressed each other urgently.

I rose in bed, ecto-mist rising with me, seeping up from the sheets and the carpet fibers like summer mist—sweet orange and vivid purple. My doorknob glowed like a glass gem. A heavy trap beat boomed beyond it.

The boys sucked at each other's necks and pulled off their shirts, their clothes disappearing into bursts of electric glitter as they left their skin. One pushed the other into the wall and started to bite his flesh.

"Can you guys find a better room?" I asked as they became increasingly naked.

"Can *you*?" the headband retorted, then went back to kissing his boyfriend before saying, "You don't own every realm."

He made a good point. The wardrobe, the mirror, the painting of that white church. None of it was mine.

The 808s made the floor wobble so hard the horseshoe above my door went from facing up to facing down.

It happens sometimes, that sentient ghosts use rooms and then leave. I assume the two boys died in that state—having sex—and I guess that would mean they're drawn to the loud music and sexual energy of party settings as they bleed from one world to the next.

I sank back into my body, curled up, and tried to fall asleep again, feeling jealous and alone.

⁘

The lesson I learned is I will never take alcohol from Grady again, because it straight knocked me out, and my stomach is twisting with some poison that hits the back of my throat like vomit.

There's a buzzing in the bathroom. Benji's electric razor fell behind the toilet paper stand and is vibrating across the floor. I put it back in place. A cockroach skitters across the tile. I run out to grab one gym shoe, kill it, and flush it.

My head's still pounding all the way down the staircase. Cups everywhere in the kitchen. A pizza box in the middle of the kitchen floor, with no pizza in it. The sweaty smell from some athletic boy who neglected a shower still lingers in the leather of the couch.

Benji made a mess of this place. I run back upstairs to his room, which has a corny yellow OFF-LIMITS road sign. Funny how it doesn't stop me from banging on the door and flinging it open. "I hope you're not expecting me to clean all this u—"

"Can you fuckin' knock?" he groans, tired and angry. He bucks in bed, pulling the cover over someone's head. A girl. All I catch of her is a nest of brown hair disappearing underneath the blanket.

"Shit—sorry." I close the door as fast as possible.

Wow. *Wow. Okay.*

Benji's always with a different girl, so I'm not surprised. Just disgusted.

Downstairs, I fill garbage bags with Solo cups and paper plates. I sweep the crumbs and go out to the patio.

I wish the night Sawyer came to my patio felt like a fever dream, but the sound of Sawyer's head slamming against the glass is programmed into my memory. Like every piece of window was at risk of breaking under the force of his skull. I can't go to sleep at night without hearing that glass shatter.

I'd guess it's about forty-five degrees. Our plant that looks like a sad mushroom and our crotons are grayish-brown husks. A fiddle-leaf fig is slowly decaying. Those never stay alive longer than a year.

The breeze blows Mom's teacup wind chimes into an ominous jingle. The camera was above the door last I knew, two nights ago, but now it's gone missing, with four holes in its place.

There's a ghoul under the oak tree in my backyard, hiding its smile behind the maple leaves.

I rush inside and shut the door. It's still watching. Like a sadist seeking revenge. There are eyes, actually. Inside the recesses of the head, where the eyes seem burned out by hot coals, are glowing white circles.

I pull out my phone. The iSpot app shows feedback from the security cameras. Front door, living room . . . and the third is now in Benji's room. The feedback is of the girl who was in his bed, dressed and up, running around the room, searching for things in a panic. I recognize her fleshy thighs, always in jean shorts, and her horse-girl hair. Laura Pearson.

"Oh my God."

Chad Roberts's girlfriend. My nemesis's girlfriend slept with my brother. It's the kind of juicy gossip I'd relish if I were more vindictive or plugged into high school drama.

The only time I can recall Laura being at my house is at a post-track-meet chiller from the two months in the semester Benji and I ran last year. Eight jocks played beer pong and talked in the kitchen while I stood by the counter, eating nachos.

Chad Roberts pulled apple juice out of our fridge and let it waterfall into his mouth.

I said, "I can get you a cup."

He kept drinking and made an *aaah* sound when he was finished.

Laura appeared, falling all over him. "Are you drinking all his juice? Stop being such a bully!" She was laughing through it, popping gum and pushing hair out of her face.

"It's a free country," Chad said. "And I'm a guest."

"Exactly," I said. "You're a guest. Benji?"

Benji came over from the beer pong table, looking slightly dazed, a little buzzed.

"Why did you invite St. Clair people to our house?" I asked.

Chad snickered. "Jesus. Racist, much?"

"If the name of the school can be equated to whiteness, there's probably a problem with the school."

"Using big words like *equated* doesn't make you sound smarter."

Chad and Laura laughed.

Benji waved a hand. "Jake, maybe rather than cause a scene, you could try to get along with people for once."

He watched Laura for her reaction, as if her approval of his statement mattered, and then dropped his gaze sadly as she fell into Chad's arms.

✣

Over the weekend it was hard to do anything, but I also couldn't sleep. I deserved a nap after cleaning our entire house. Mom didn't notice a thing had changed when she returned.

Normally, I try to stay awake at school, except in psych, which is a great place to doze off. Mr. Morrison plays documentaries every day to get out of teaching, so I take a snooze.

My head is fully in the notebook, my eyes almost closed, when a voice jolts me awake.

"S'cuse me."

I suck in my drool and yank my head off my desk. The cold flash from the documentary blinks on me and frames the outline of the person who's spoken. He's standing in the aisle in a patient way. It's not Mr. Morrison—it's a student.

"Just . . . try'na get by."

"Oh." I take my book bag from the aisle and put it under my desk.

It's still dark, but I could swear it's another Black boy who's taking the seat behind me.

Another one of us at St. Clair?

"Thanks," he whispers into my shoulder.

I can't tell from his voice, and it would be awkward to turn around. Part of me wants to look back and shake his hand. Another part of me is on the defense . . . What if he's one of those Black kids who hates other Black kids and is an asshole to me? That's the last thing I need in my life right now.

⁘

Grady ambushes me in the bathroom after class when I'm taking a piss.

"Dude, what the hell happened?" He's angry for some reason, and one of his elbows is resting on the flush valve of the next urinal.

"Grady . . . please. That's so unsanitary."

"I texted you so much, and you just ghosted me, man! Why?"

"Sorry, I was asleep." *And dealing with more pressing matters than that stupid party.*

"Asleep? We agreed to do the party. And you fell asleep?" His face is tomato red as he glares at me, and it looks like tears might spill out of his beady eyes—some weird combination of anger and sadness. "So I got a ride all the way out there and just had to go home thirty minutes later because your brother doesn't fucking know me?"

"I never agreed to anything, Grady—"

"That's not fair, bro! This was my chance!"

"Your chance for what? To be friends with my brother?" I zip up my pants and walk around him to the sinks. "I fell asleep. I got tired from that alcohol *you* gave me. Sorry."

"Are you serious right now?" He's still watching me even as I wash my hands. "You act like you're spaced out all the time, Jake. I think you're just a horrible friend."

He storms out of the bathroom.

Well, I guess it's over. Maybe it's for the best. Grady's just been waiting for a forbidden adventure to my house all this time. I never got much from the friendship anyway.

Then again, am I a horrible friend? Maybe that's why I don't have more of them.

The stall doors open while I'm leaning on a sink, thinking about if I'm wrong and if there's something I've missed.

"That sounded messy." It's the other Black kid. Caramel skin; skin clearer than mine; haircut fresh, short, and even. He's an inch taller, and his sweater hugs his big arms.

"It's okay. I didn't like that guy anyway." I catch myself in the shiny silver paper-towel dispenser, where a dent distorts my reflection.

I can't ever seem to use one paper towel only, so I take down four. The boy turns off his sink and takes two off my hands.

And then he dries his hands. And holds one out to me. "Allister."

"Jake Livingston."

Oh, God. Your full name? For what reason?

When our hands touch, green light blossoms between our thumbs, curls around our fingers, and spirals up our arms. Like a breath of ivy creating one aura between us. Pink flowers sprout to dress the vine and . . . I can honestly say, in all my years as a medium, I have never seen a garden grow between me and another person.

When we break hands, the aura travels to his head to shape into a misty wreath of soft pink.

What does someone have to think about themselves to wear a crown in their aura? To be a king?

"So, you're new?" I ask.

"Yeah. I was supposed to start last month, but there was a problem in admissions. They put me on a wait list but then forgot to *notify* me that I got in. My dad's an ethical hacker. Builds security systems for network penetration purposes. He went digging and found out my family's contact info had been knocked off their mailing list. Had to nudge them twice to get a response."

"That's . . . awful."

I face myself in the mirror and remember how much I hate being the one Black person in every classroom. I never sit with this feeling, because my declining GPA is stressful enough on top of the fact that I'm confused by how to make friends I really like. And maybe . . . just maybe, I'd want a boyfriend at some point. The only issue is another boy would have to like me back.

Allister's been watching me like he knows what I'm thinking.

It's awkward, but in a good way. For now, it seems like I can be myself.

"Your teeth are very white," I tell him.

He laughs. It's a miracle I made him do that. Usually I'm too awkward to say anything funny.

As the bell rings, he rolls his sweater sleeve back over a silver watch. "Welp. Guess we should get to class now that the bell's already rung. Nice meeting you, Jake."

He winks at me, so fast I wonder if I imagined it. He waltzes out of the bathroom, determined to get somewhere more important. Did this whole interaction not make his heart hammer a million beats a minute? I guess it's just me.

·:·

I think of him on my daily walk through the stacks in the library as I munch on my sandwich.

Allister . . . what a name. Like an alchemist from an era long past.

How long would it take to call Allister a friend? I don't want to rush things, but I feel comfortable with him.

There's a flash of movement at the end of the stack. A blond-haired person disappearing around the corner.

Sawyer.

I follow him as he walks down the next aisle. From behind I can tell that it's Sawyer, because he's stuck in that hoodie-jeans combo. He's stiff but unrushed as he walks, his feet nearly invisible and landing on nothing.

He stops once he reaches the end of the aisle, and I pause behind him, fearing he'll turn around and do something . . . shoot me, somehow, with a phantom weapon.

Instead, he begins to float, slowly, like an angel, toward the ceiling. Up and up, through the lights and through to the next floor. Like an elevator.

I bolt down the aisle and slide around the corner, the bookshelf labels flying in colors around me. I bust through the library doors. Someone bumps into my shoulder on their way through the lobby.

"Hey!"

"Sorry . . . sorry . . ."

The hinges rattle behind me as I dive into the stairwell and jump the steps to the third floor.

Third floor. An empty tunnel of lockers. And then, a red and black smoke trail disappearing behind the corner down the hall.

"Where the fuck are you going?"

I keep on running, the straps of my book bag heavy on my shoulders, the weight of the whole thing stabbing my lower back. I have to catch him, to know what he wants.

The lights go out, leaving a darkness packed in by sunlight at the ends of the hallway.

Gasping from the classrooms—everyone is thrilled for the moment of sudden darkness.

The lights flicker back on, blinking up the hallway, like something's turning them on one by one. I yank my phone out of my pocket and click on the flashlight—a source of light to keep myself here should another outage come.

I find my feet and start running.

Sawyer's waiting for me around the next corner. He's there for a moment and then phasing through the door up to the roof.

I run forward, bum-rush the push handle, and mount the staircase. My hand trails the cold railing as I jump the steps, the flashlight beam skipping along the walls.

I throw open the door to the roof, and the wind snatches the last bit of breath out of my throat. From here you can usually see St. Clair Middle past the quad out front of school. The rugby field and tennis courts out back. The skyline in the distance to the east, the sea of trees interspersed with the city. It's too foggy to see far beyond the roof today. And no one is up here.

No one except Sawyer.

Sawyer, standing with his back turned, watching the horizon.

He steps and steps again across the pavement, leaving a red trail in his wake. His aura, red with notes of black, bleeds from his ears, seeps from his skin. A dark, horrible color shaping the energy of the atmosphere around him. A cloud of smoke and dust forms a snake, which curls around his neck; and then wasps, which buzz around his head; and then a demon, which jumps back from his body with its wrists curled and then scuttles back in, quick as a spider down a hole.

What's happening? He's like the rainfall—there, and then not. Fluid, and solid.

He stops at the barrier railing—the only thing between a ledge and a drop off the building. "Would you say you hate school?"

"Leave me alone." I close the distance cautiously.

"Would you say you hate your classmates and teachers and the way that they've treated you?" His Southern accent is old and haunting.

Stronger now. Come on, Jake. "Leave. Me. ALONE."

"Why would I do that?" Sawyer laughs—like a child at first, and then the sound deepens into the laughter of a man. "I don't want to! I don't want to!" But the voice is still that of a child.

The clouds darken over the school, threatening a sudden storm, and I notice a bloodstain on the right side of his head, where his hair shatters in a spray of crusted blond across his forehead.

My feet start sliding from under me, pulling me toward him, and I slap the pavement with my butt.

Sawyer sics on me like a predator. His aura pulls me up like hooks under my armpits, and then I'm dangling there, right in front of him, slightly above him. Gone are the blue eyes from before. Black depths have filled their place. A vacuum, powered by his face, rips the air, oxygen, and life from the marrow of my bones. My muscles ache, and I collapse, drained, exhausted, dizzy.

I want to grab him by the hair and smash his head into the railing. Kill him, right here, right now.

But I'm ... too ... weak ... to move? Can't ... touch ... I can feel the ... Can't see the ... Can't ... breathe ...

A hot wind thrashes me in the face and spins me through the air, so I land like a hammer on my stomach and chin, gray spots exploding everywhere.

"What's wrong?" His voice is in my head and seeping from the cracks in the stones, the fountain, the foundation of the school. Possessing dead world and the living world all at once.

I cough my way to healthy breaths and find my feet. "What do you want from me?"

Back away from the ledge. I've gotten closer to it. I think he wanted to throw me off.

"What do you want from me?"

He's blinking in and out of existence again, fading and returning like he did on my patio—one moment a fully formed boy, and the next, a suggestion of a figure, a see-through screen with the trees in full view behind him.

"What do children want from toys?" He's coming toward me.

"To ... To play with them?" I don't know why I'm answering his question. My mind is upside down. There's a roaring in my head. A rumbling in my stomach.

My energy returns, little by little. Dizzy and dreary, but I can stand up straight, at least. My thoughts are decomposing, and the paving is gray, and everything is gray.

"I'm *banishing* you." It weeps out of me. "I said I'm banishing you."

"I heard you." His voice is strong enough to lift my head to face him.

In the smoke of his aura rise striking snakes, a diving hawk, a swarm of flies. Temporary visions of predators and pests jumping at the air and escaping through it.

Everything I know about ghosts feels somehow irrelevant now.

Sawyer levitates, veins popping with red energy, the aura lifting him into a state of fragile flight.

"How does it feel to be caught in the middle of something that has nothing to do with you?" His voice is like ten voices from ten rooms of hell. "*Do I hear a question from Matteo Mooney?* Matteo wants to know—Did you feel bad for me, Jake? When you saw how I died?"

"What?"

"*Answer the boy, answer the boy!*" says a voice like a horrible jingle from a circus intercom, and I am on a carousel of doubt.

Did I feel bad for Matteo? Of course. He got murdered by a floating knife. That's fucking awful. But what happened between them had nothing to do with me, and I fail to see why anything between them would concern me.

"You didn't feel sorry for him," Sawyer says, and suddenly he's on the ground again, the aura sucking back into his pores and follicles, burying under his skin. It's a flush in his pale cheeks, a glow in his pimples. "Maybe you shouldn't have so much power if you can't stop people from dying."

"What are you talking about? Why are you bothering me?"

"Because maybe you should give up your body to someone who knows how to use it." He tilts his head at me, robot-like, his eyes pure math and no empathy. "Yes, yours would be a good body for me."

It must be his final statement, because he's walking away. A breeze whistles harshly in his wake, spinning up a storm of leaves. The bloody side of his head folds in and out of the air as it moves and he moves.

No motion in his arms or upper body—just a hunch in his shoulders. He takes baby steps forward until he phases through the brick wall, gone as quickly as he appeared.

JAKE

There are less than a thousand students at St. Clair, but the hallways always feel tense and overcrowded.

There's a rising commotion of voices responding to some shouting. Up ahead, more people are gathered in one circle than usual. There's a fight going on . . . There's a fight going on? That's rare for St. Clair, to have people with their phones held up in a circle like this.

I run up to the crowd, eager to see two people beating the shit out of each other. I guess it's just cathartic to see something new.

What I find are Benji and Chad in hand-to-hand combat. Benji throwing a punch into Chad's nose, drawing blood. Chad grabbing Benji's shirt to throw him into a locker.

Someone blocks my view and snaps to get my attention. "While I would have preferred if you came to me personally, I'm glad I know now." Mahalia. She's always put together and smiling, but today her eyes are flames behind her high-perched glasses, her red lips pursed with indignation. "Just tell me, Jake. Why? Why did you upload this?"

She holds out her phone to me like it's a dirty artifact she'll have to drop in a plastic bag. A video plays from . . . my abandoned TikTok account? My profile picture is the one from my school ID card. A year old. I barely do pictures, and I definitely don't do social media. I'd much rather zone out to an album or draw something. I haven't logged into that account in months.

So then how did the video from our security feed get on there and get seven hundred views overnight?

"I . . . I didn't do this," I stammer.

"Um, Jake?" Mahalia's eyes widen with a slow nod. "It looks like you did!"

If I wanted to take a dig at my brother, or his life, I wouldn't have done it like this.

Mahalia's not even paying attention as Benji punches Chad in the stomach behind her. She takes a deep breath and blinks at the ceiling. "Of course I knew how he was. Everyone knows Benji Livingston is a narcissist playboy. It was dumb to give him so much of me. I admit it." She looks at me. "I'm confused by you. I thought you were a nice kid. I know we don't talk like that, but this hurts. And it's embarrassing as hell. Why?"

"I didn't . . ." I know I'll sound like an idiot, so I just shut up after that.

She's perplexed. "How's it from your account, then? Why would he say that you did?"

"He did?"

"He's very convinced that you did it to drive a wedge between me and him. Not that I'm ever hearing him out again. Because even if you did, it doesn't change what he did."

Laura's red face and wild hair appear in the gaps between bystanders' heads. "Stop fighting!" she screams at Benji and Chad. "You guys, stop fighting!"

Mahalia rolls her eyes at her. "Is *that* what I'm up against? He could've chosen *anyone*. Laura's not even AP! How long have you known about this, Jake?"

"Mahalia, I haven't known—I swear, please listen to me. I ignore my brother! I ignore everything he does. It wasn't . . ."

It wasn't me. I couldn't have committed a crime in my sleep. It's not possible unless my astral body took the camera down. Even if it were possible (which it might be), why would my astral body do something so chaotic?

Everyone is turning to look at me like I'm the one who started the fight. These kids whose names I only know because they're always so loud when talking to each other—Katie, Chip, Steven.

I must've stayed logged in from my phone, and some cruel person chose to download the video and upload it to TikTok. Anyone with access to the phone and my fingerprint could've done it while I was sleeping.

S.A.D. The killer who drew his name in the air over Matteo Mooney. Who drew the same thing on the wall of my house so the blood of his victim simmered in the plaster. I still see it when I walk to the kitchen or living room, though Benji and Mom say they can't.

Sawyer's initials may just be imprinted onto my psyche and affecting the way I see the real world. He vandalized my book because he knew it would embarrass me in class. He leaked my brother's sex video because . . . it would embarrass me at school, and at home.

"Jake, are you zoning out?" Mahalia's waving in front of my face. The tension relaxes from her shoulders, and she puts her hand on my shoulder. "Not to tell you what to do, but if your friends really did this, then you may want to *unfriend* them? And clear your name to your brother, since he thinks it was you."

With that, she walks around me to get to class, heels clicking with determination.

Principal Ross arrives a second later, charging like a bull toward Benji. "Hey! Hey! Hey!"

He rips him away, and Chad collapses on one knee, blood trickling over his chin. "St-st-stay away from her."

The principal storms off with Benji's elbow in his grip.

My stomach hurts. It feels like I did this, even though I know it's more likely Sawyer uploaded it. Right after he reached one hand out of dead world and ripped the camera down.

Sawyer is hyperaware of the inner workings of my life and gets satisfaction from poking at it, probably in hopes the whole thing will topple over, because it's fun and it feeds his weird obsession with seeing chaos in his wake.

How does it feel to be caught in the middle of something that has nothing to do with you?

✢

On the bus that afternoon, someone stares at me. Across the aisle, perfectly upright, smiling deadly. They watch me through the narrow channel of Ponce de Leon Avenue, under the grove of Fairview and Lullwater. They smile at me, their head tilting slowly, closing the distance between us as the bus runs from the suburbs into the city.

I face them and find a skinny man reading a book in the fold-down seat, one leg crossed over the other, paying me no attention.

I imagined it.

My reflection in the window dazes me. I didn't brush my teeth long enough or wipe the crust from my eyes.

I pull the wire down at Euclid and leap over a puddle to reach the sidewalk. Trash water splashes up in the big wheels, and when it's gone, there's someone behind it charging at me from across the street, a knife held up and ready to swing down.

I shrink into the bus stop and blink.

It was nothing. Only a telephone pole standing at the inter-weaving roads and tram tracks.

The midafternoon sun threatens darkness. I hustle past the murals, thrift stores, and restaurants, my destination past a street performer and his raggedy dog. A little booth between the alleyways, tucked in so you can barely find it.

I go inside, past a curtain of beads. Candlelight burns softly over the glass displays. Bracelets and necklaces, amethysts and emeralds on cords of gold. Canisters of shea butter, books on voodoo and Yoruba.

Ms. Josette is standing in the walkway at the back of her shop. A green-and-gold gown shapes her like a serpent. Her dreads are long and freshly twisted, their sheen reflecting in the candlelight.

"It's funny," she says, her voice like an oracle. "Something told me I'd be visited by a certain Jake Joseph Livingston today."

"Hi, Ms. Josette."

She's still and brooding, eyes wide as the moon, mouth pursed with disapproval. "You ignored my last call."

"Oh." I laugh nervously. "My bad. I don't talk to anybody, really. I've been trying to get better about that."

She comes toward me, her gait languid and graceful—a swag too tough to cross—and pulls me in for a tight hug. "Well, at least you're here now. I'm sensing . . . *increased panic*. Fear for your life."

Amazing how she does that. "Something like that."

"Come to the back."

The chamber has an intricate Kashmir carpet, with flowers, pinwheels, and faces in the patterns. I sit on the floor and rest my elbows on the low table. The alphabet forms a rainbow shape in the wood. There are numbers underneath, and GOOD BYE is carved into the bottom.

I grab a pillow and hug it to my lap.

Ms. Josette plops into a green armchair across from me and pours a cup of tea.

"I'm only hard on you because I want to know you're safe," she says. "How's it been, managing the perceptions?"

"Fine, mostly. I'm better at it now. Better than I used to be."

"No ghouls hanging out in your bedroom?"

"I saw one in my neighbor's yard. Well, I saw one in my yard today too."

Josette slows the kettle to a drip. "That doesn't sound good. Usually they show up to the homes where all the joy has gone missing." She puts the kettle down, crosses her legs. "What's going on, Jake?"

"I . . . I don't know." *I guess there's no joy in my house.* "It's not just the ghouls. I'm afraid something else is after me. I kind of feel like I'm fine, and it can't really hurt me, but then I feel like it can. And it's just waiting for the right moment, or slowly planning my demise. A ghost. A vengeful one who's trying to haunt me for some reason, and I don't know why, because I haven't done anything to this person. I never knew this person."

There's a moon and a sun carved into this table too. A YES and a NO.

"In what ways is it haunting you?"

"Showing up at my house. On the patio. And at school, in the library. It shows up, and it doesn't usually do anything, but today it did. It was floating through the walls, and I chased it up to the roof. And it told me . . ."

Flute music is playing from somewhere. A lullaby replacing the memories in my brain. That conversation with Sawyer was barely comprehensible. I don't remember what he said, because he seemed to be talking over me. I can't trust that it really happened, or that there is any reason to be here.

What has Sawyer really done to me?

Desecrated the book. Creepy, but that could have been ignored, and if I had ignored it, maybe the ecto-mist wouldn't have pushed me toward the scene of the crime. The mist eavesdrops on that part of my brain I try to tune out—the one that wants to know more about Sawyer. Who was he before he shot up his school? What drove him to do it? What *was* the motive? And why is he so interested in me?

"It told you what, Jake?" Ms. Josette says.

I forgot I'd started a sentence. "I don't know. He goes wherever he does. He does whatever he wants. He's not looping, not in the regular way, and not in the extended way either. He's not trapped in the moment he died. He's not trapped with the gun that killed him or in the confines of the building. He's not doomed at all. He has free rein."

Her expression is grave. "It's possible. Ghosts who haven't crossed realms by way of freak accident may arrive in dead world completely free of a loop at all."

"What if they crossed by suicide? Does that count as accidental?"

She closes her eyes and shakes her head slowly. "Suicide interrupts the whole scheme." She grabs a Newton's cradle off a side table—a pendulum with five balls. Each time the ball at one end swings down, it triggers the one on the other side. "The ball on one end is the Here—the real world—and the ball on the other is the After. The balls in between are dead world—the Divide. Ghosts may be closer to living humans, like us, if they weren't kicked as far toward the After as this ball over here.

They remain stuck, but at different levels of awareness. Based on their individual circumstances."

The clicking balls remind me of that ticking I heard in my house that night. "What makes the difference?" I ask. "I mean, how could a ghost stay close to life if they're dead? Why?"

"Various reasons. Any reason. The universe is *supposed* to have a fixed relationship with human life. Our life spans are *meant* to be programmed, predetermined from the day we're born. So, when a freak accident happens, it upsets the schema. The universe can't process it, and it stores that person's life as a glitch."

The pendulum swings and clicks behind her voice. "But a sudden death brought on by a person's own will, of their own autonomy? It's complicated. It could outglitch the glitch. Say the person's suicide is driven by low self-esteem or hopelessness. Well, I'd expect that person to loop. To feel a loss of control that *carries over* into the Divide.

"But! Say the person harms themselves as a means of harming others—to make their loved ones mourn for them, or to make someone pay. Well, they'd cross the realm motivated by vengeance."

"And the vengeance would . . . tether them to the living world."

"Vengeance tends to tether you to things you're meant to forget. A spirit like the one you're describing could very well have calculated the circumstances of its own death long before Death itself had time to catch up."

The dead roses hanging upside down from the corners keep reminding me of Sawyer's aura. The bleeding, decaying continuum of red. And the wraiths, jumping out in visions of black. Birds and wasps.

I rush to the bookshelf, snatch up a deck of wraith cards, and spill them out on the table.

"By all means." Josette sits across from me.

I spread around the cards and survey the inkblots of animals with their descriptions underneath.

Spider

the curdling isolation of neglect unfurls
inside you like eight legs

Hawk

you foresee a perceptive foe with
a wise and deadly presence

Wasp

you may become a victim of someone's
misdirected vengeance

"Wraiths," Ms. Josette says. "The most phony of the phony things you might ever see."

"So, they're not real?" I ask. "They're really just projections?"

"Projections by the ghost, exacerbated by your own fear. It's what the experienced haunter will use to frighten you into a state of anxiety so that it can use that anxiety to frighten you even more."

There was something else I saw—like a demon of ash, running from and back into his body. "Is there one of these for, like, a demon figure?"

Ms. Josette flicks her wrist, and a vortex of ecto-mist separates the cards into a perfect circle, leaving one in the center. "Derelict."

I snatch the card off the table and study the hunched, emaciated figure.

DERELICT
*you fear your body will soon
be taken from you*

"Would a ghost who projects this want to possess my body?" I ask.

From the size of her bulging eyes, it looks an awful lot like a yes. "First things first." Her tone is somber. "You control you. Your body is your body, and you remind yourself of that every day. Something like what you're describing wants to colonize your sense of self. So you set a boundary. In short, you tell it to buzz off." She leaps up, comes around the table, sandwiches my face between her hands, and forces my spine to straighten. "Don't let it get to you, and it might just leave you alone."

"Is that . . . all it takes?"

"It takes belief." She turns abruptly and traverses the room, her gown trailing behind her. "It takes *self-esteem*. It takes knowing that your reality is not up for debate. And last but not least? It takes *assertiveness*. Say its name if you know it and tell it to get lost. You want it away from you bad enough? It works."

I tried. It didn't work. "What if it doesn't work?"

"Well, then you may have to work on your directness, or your self-esteem. Check on your smells too. Smells that they remember fondly will vitalize ghosts with energy. The wrong ones ward them off."

I always burn the wilderness and wildflowers incense in my

room. But maybe Sawyer likes that smell too. Maybe he's drawn to the forest, or nature, or maybe he just likes some of the same stuff I do.

If Sawyer is responsible for everything that's been happening, and if he wants to possess me, he'd do it by bothering me first. Toying with my sense of safety, weaseling his way in, and destroying my morale. Sawyer has a hit list and the intention of possessing me, both.

I stand up abruptly. "Thank you, Ms. Josette."

She doesn't move immediately—she's not finished. "Gone so soon? You dropped a lot on me in a moment."

"You helped me. I should finish my work from the weekend—there's a lot."

If the point is to reduce Sawyer's presence in my mind, then I have to take my mind off of him. And being around all this metaphysical stuff isn't exactly helping. Here, my whole existence feels tied to my curse.

Ms. Josette follows me to the curtain of beads in front of the door. "Is everything gonna be all right, Jake?"

"Yeah, I'll be good!"

I don't want her to worry.

But I feel inadequate. Not good enough. Not fearless enough. Definitely not confident enough. Most of the time I'm afraid of my teachers and peers judging me, or of being beat up by my brother, or of disappointing Mom.

I'm just a regular kid. I save my birthday money and buy one new thing every six months. Headphones, a bow tie, a mini trampoline. I become obsessed with that new thing and throw all my time and emotions into it.

Maybe that's because I don't want to face my emotions, or

the truth—that I don't believe in myself very much at all. I don't know what there is to believe in.

But if I accept that, it means I've already lost.

⁘

Benji's in the driveway when I get home. He's rolled my book cart outside the house. A book is burning in a trash can, and Benji's smashing my incense jar with a baseball bat. The glass goes everywhere.

"What are you *doing*?" I scream, running up to the driveway from the street.

"Destroying everything you love, just like you did to me." He breaks my elephant with no remorse.

"Why?"

"Because you took a video of me having sex with someone and then leaked it to the internet, you sicko."

"I didn't leak that video. Why would I do that? That would be disgusting."

Chad bruised his eye up so bad he can barely open it, so it's hard to see if he's even looking at me. "So you're saying someone else at the party hacked into our security-camera system and decided to make a porno of me and Laura."

"Yes, that's exactly what happened."

"Who did it?"

"Sawyer."

"Who?"

"Sawyer Doon."

He blinks. "Who?"

"The ghost." I begin to pace. "The ghost who wrote the initials on the wall—I told you. He's done other things too. Wrote a bunch of bloody letters in my book and showed up in the library.

He's been following me around. He's been on the patio, he's been at school, and *he's* the one who moved the camera into your room to cause some sort of scandal—"

"Jake—okay, stop." Benji groans, closing his eyes. "Jake, I've really never heard someone blame all their shitty behavior on ghosts except for you. You have a mental illness. You really do."

He may be right. "This wasn't my fault." My voice is a whisper, diminished.

"I think you want to get noticed. That's what the ghost thing is. You want to be special and mysterious and *alternative*, but you're just weird and need help."

"Of course I need help . . . and you're no help and never have been." Tears tremble in my throat. "And you treat girls horribly too. Maybe whoever did it knew you should be exposed for the scumbag you are. Maybe *you* need help."

Benji doesn't move, but anger seethes in his eyes and his chest. I know it could go either way. He could knock my head off or walk away.

After a standoff, he throws the bat at my feet. "I hope the ghost kills you."

The pile of salt from my incense jar sweeps into the wind as the weapon rolls in a circle, and Benji walks into the house, slamming the door behind him.

SAWYER

November 1

Dear Diary,

Family bonding, for Momma, is when she's not involved, and instead it's me and a man who's older. It's why she always wanted Bill to help me build a tree house but didn't want to help me herself.

I always hear her in the other room on the phone with Uncle Rod. "Talk to him? I think he just needs someone to talk to."

My dad is gone, so family bonding amounts to weekend shooting trips with Uncle Rod. He leaves his cooler open so he can drink and shoot at the same time.

The Hapeville doctors were explicitly clear about me not having access to weapons or proximity to mind-altering substances. I don't think Momma was listening. Maybe she doesn't care.

I took the military-standard Mossberg, and Rod took the classic Remington. Tactical shotguns are fun to play with, even if our targets are just barrels and bottles. Why, if there are deer, rabbits, and fox in the forest, do we shoot at soda cans and beer? Seems futile not to make another animal our prey, cut it up, and eat it.

"I was worried when you were in the hospital last summer," he told me. He put his gun down, sat on the log with his elbows on his knees. A real bonding moment. He took a graceless swig of beer and told me, "Depression ain't permanent. Probably because your scumbag dad left you. You'll get over it."

Funny. Bill and Rod seemed like great friends when they were both here.

"You wanna know why I gave you that gun?" Rod said. "Why I brought you out here? It's 'cause a man needs to feel that kind of power in his hands to know what he's capable of. My uncle, your great-uncle Jimmy Beasley, thought there was something wrong with me because my earliest friends were girls. Told me I would have to get into sports. Told him the tetherball court was where the girls was, not the baseball court." Rod laughed and looked sadly at the pine needles. "Just liked girls real young and wanted to be around 'em—no harm in that. Startin' early. You had sex yet, Sawyer?"

I shook my head. I haven't thought much of it, much less tried to have it. But I was so intrigued by his tangent. It made no sense.

He ran to set his empty Heineken on a log, baggy overalls threatening to slip off his skinny shoulders. He's long in shape, but with a round belly. He tried to shoot the Heineken but kept missing, until finally, he screamed, "FUCK!"

Red-faced, he dropped the gun and dragged his fingers down his forehead. He was so furious with himself, and I understood why. I'd hate myself too if my whole personality was based on shooting guns and I couldn't even do that right.

JAKE

In the days following my visit with Ms. Josette, I observed that the best way to trade in fear for joy was to think of Allister Burroughs. I feel ridiculous letting someone get in my head so fast, but he *has* smiled when we've passed each other in the hallway ever since that first day.

And finally, there's another eleventh grader who gets what it's like to swim in a pool not made for you.

Today when I walked into class, he was too busy doodling to see me take my seat in front of him. Mr. Morrison started the documentary and instantly fell asleep at his desk.

I'm awake, but barely, until Allister taps me on the shoulder and passes me a note, which I unfold in a hurry.

Cupcakes or brownies? His writing is impeccable, and honestly, that's a turn-on.

Heart racing, I pick up my pen to respond. Everyone in the vicinity is, thankfully, minding their own business.

Depends on what flavor cupcake and the fudginess of the brownie.

Cupcake vanilla with cream cheese frosting. Brownie oozing fudge.

I don't like it too gooey. I prefer a moist cake texture. Cupcake.

Sounds like you've never had the right fudge experience.

The smile that marks my face feels more powerful than me. But I also feel sad and overwhelmed. The darkness of this classroom, where everyone's half asleep, is keeping this little rendezvous a secret. If someone caught me getting giggly over these notes, they'd get the wrong impression and . . . well, I don't know what would happen. St. Clair assumes everyone to be straight, and these notes feel secretive and scandalous.

Maybe I'm reading into things.

I'm sure there's a super-fudgey brownie somewhere out there that would make me change my mind.

We should find it.

My heart starts to beat loud enough to hear. Is this what they call flirting? More importantly: Is this an invitation to hang out? I write it down and cross it out. I can't take it too far. Of course Allister couldn't *like me* like me. Of course he wouldn't be into boys that way.

Pizza or pasta?

Pizza all the way. Favorite color?

Emerald green. You?

Pink.

Hot pink?

Soft pink.

Soft pink . . . that sounds kind of . . .

I feel a pair of eyes on me, which draw my focus to Chad Roberts one seat over. He's half asleep, half watching my business in a way that is not at all subtle.

Allister taps me under the arm with a new piece of paper. He's so eager to talk, he hasn't even given me time to respond, and he obviously doesn't care who sees.

Is your next class skippable?

I don't skip.

Oh, so you're a nerd.

No . . . I just don't want to get in trouble.

That's what being a nerd is, nerd.
Meet me after class.

After the bell rings, I wait for him outside the classroom door. Allister walks out after most everyone else, like he purposely kept me waiting.

He passes me, and then dramatically turns around. "Oh! Hi—didn't see you there."

I want to smile, but I don't. "Yes, you did." I pull the strings on my book bag and fall into step with him. "So, you're a skipper? Didn't see that coming. You seem so . . . *erudite*."

"As if it's possible to wear this uniform and not come off that way. I'm not a skipper—not by identity. Just a kid enjoying the benefits of being a new kid while they last. I still don't know my way around. Can you show me?"

He gives me a wink and pops his gum. I can smell the Winterfresh from here.

"What's my excuse?" I press closer to him so our conversation is quieted by the hallway traffic—just between us. "I've never missed a day of class in my life."

He shrugs. "You're living a little?"

He makes a point. I'm always getting called out or kicked out. What's showing up worth, anyway? Does it matter? I wear my uniform, stay quiet, and don't cause a scene. And even then, someone's always watching me, looking for a reason to single me out or screw me over. Maybe following the rules isn't keeping me as safe here as I thought.

Allister nods at a couple making out hot and heavy against a locker and whispers, "Gross."

Because they're kissing in public? Or because they're a boy and a girl?

In the stairwell, he slides down the railing, almost running into a guy who moves aside for him. "Look alive, bro—my bad!" He meets the landing in a clumsy one-footed hop, his tie flying behind him like a cape. He does a twirl around someone else. "Excuse me. Yes, pardon me."

I weave and walk, chasing him down the next flight of stairs, afraid I could lose him.

People adjust their steps to make room for him. People never move when I say excuse me, probably because I don't speak loud enough, or maybe I don't move with as much confidence.

He glances over his shoulder and reaches back like he wants me to take his hand. Then it turns into a *follow me* gesture.

Did I imagine an invitation to hold hands? Maybe I'm just crazy. Maybe I'm the only boy within a thousand-mile radius who thinks of other boys that way.

The back door takes us to a small staircase, which takes us to an old asphalt basketball court. Its hoop is just a rim without a net. It looks like a relic from a neighborhood that existed here before St. Clair.

Allister slides down the railing again. I want to try, but I know I'll bust my ass.

"Aren't you worried we'll be caught on camera?" I ask.

"Nope!" He jumps and slaps the rim and lands, backing away, balanced on his feet. "Aren't you worried you think vanilla cupcakes are better than fudge brownies?"

It's eleven in the morning. The sun is out, the leaves sweeping the concrete in dramatic typhoons. Something about the chaos is romantic—maybe because it threatens to blow us away. Allister turns around and draws closer to me as we cross the court. We're headed toward the residential roads, which wind murkily under and through deciduous trees. Elm and beech leaves bunch at the curb like wet laundry, in shades of bronze, cantaloupe, and blood.

Allister leaps over a root as we cross a patch of grass. "So, I heard Mr. Morrison and Ms. Kingston are always seen entering campus from this way together at around two thirty p.m., her with her hair messed up, him with his tie a little loose—is that true?"

"I don't know. Kind of hard for me to follow the gossip around here."

"You mind your own business," he says. "I like that."

⁘

We hit the strip mall first. All these cute burger joints and fro-yo huts tucked between the high-rise buildings, glass-walled apartment complexes, corporate skyscrapers, multi-floor grocery stores, and trendy fast-food chains.

Sunwood is the comfortable living paradise of my dreams, and I hate that it's haunted by the whiteness of the place and my school. I hate that every four seconds I have to look behind me to see if Sawyer is sitting in the car, planning my demise.

⊹

Cake Bunny is a hut, painted green, where Allister opens the door for me.

"Thanks." The heat of the store hits hard and then cools as we approach the girl at the cashier—her name tag says SHAUNA. She's in a green bunny-ear beanie that starkly contrasts with her black bangs.

She squints at Allister and me and pops her gum with the lazy indifference of an overworked college student. "Y'all skipping school?"

"Nope," Allister says with a mischievous smile. "We're ordering two fudge brownie sundaes."

She cracks a smile because his is contagious and then taps the screen. "Two brownie fudgies. Will that be all?"

"Yup!"

Is it really that easy? Why isn't she calling the cops?

"You nervous?" he asks as we wait in the channel between the door and the tables.

"I don't know . . . I just don't want them to call my mom or anything. I feel like they're always watching me anyway."

"Who?"

"Teachers. Students." *Sawyer.*

The door opens and a cold breeze comes through the store, but nobody walks in.

"Damn ghost door!" Shauna grumbles as she leaves two tubs on the counter.

"Thank you," Allister and I say, nearly in unison, as the door taps on its frame.

Every pesky tick of strange phenomena feels like a carefully seeded message now. A message from Sawyer.

I head for a table with my sundae, and I wish that I could have my peace back. That I could sit down at a table and enjoy a sweet treat without worrying that every good thing is only temporary. Without feeling like a murderer is breathing down my neck.

⁘

Concrete turns to brick as Allister leads us from the strip mall and past the gates of Sunwood University. The quadrangle is like a medieval monastery. College students lounge in the grass, bundled in scarves and jeans, those markers of freedom. No navy blue, no stiff, shiny shoes. People are here because they want to be, not because they're trapped. I both dream of that freedom and feel like I'll never reach it.

The wind is biting. Allister seems less cold. I'm in my hood, and he's in no hat or head covering. I take note of his ears—big and quirky. And his flat-front navy shorts, which fall above the knee, forming a gap between them and his navy socks.

"Are your legs not cold?" I ask.

"Nope. I know, it's weird. But I like a brisk wind. Keeps me awake."

I don't find it weird. I don't find much weird, really.

Allister stops suddenly at a green statue in the grass—a white man on a horse. "Confederate general Buford Buck. What do you think would be the easiest way to rip this down?"

I inspect it from all sides. "Wrecking ball?"

"Come on, Miley."

"Or maybe fire to loosen the foundation and then rope to pull it down. I haven't removed many statues in my day."

He grabs one of the hooves, testing its firmness. "I love your style, Jake. Just burn it down." He pulls the lid off the sundae and shoves a spoonful into his wide mouth. "Okay, brownie time. Tell me if you change your mind."

Jackhammers and bulldozers sound off in the distance as we plop down on a bench. I squint up to watch leaves fall and settle on the bricks. "I hope a leaf doesn't get in my sundae."

"Better eat it fast to keep that from happening." He spins and crosses his legs, hovering over the dessert. "Race you to the finish."

He's devouring his with the kidlike enthusiasm of anyone eating a brownie sundae. I can't even eat mine, though. I'm laughing kind of a lot, and every spoonful gives me brain freeze, and my mouth can't handle as much as his, and he's treating this as an Olympic sport.

"Okay, okay." I swallow a glob of sweet vanilla and cough. "This hurts. You win. You're too fast."

Allister scrapes the spoon around the rim, licks it, and tosses it in the trash. His eyes smile even when his mouth doesn't. They're brown and hopeful, shaped like hickory leaves with accents near the temples.

He puts his legs down and grips the bench, smirking at me from the side. "Have I convinced you that brownie sundaes are far superior to cupcakes or whatever the hell?"

I stick my spoon deep into the ice cream, eager to match him where he is. "I think you might have convinced me."

SAWYER

November 2

Dear Diary,

It's my one-month anniversary in the free world. I've continued to shoot with Uncle Rod and stare at the ceiling. I don't do any of my homework. All of my teachers know that I'm struggling, but they continue to ask me to follow the rules.

I'm not following any rules anymore. I'm eating, and sleeping, and hiding in the shed whenever I want to. I do whatever I want. The more people ask me to do nice things, the more I want to do bad things.

Momma has forced Annie to be nicer to me. I wanted that last week but don't anymore. Sometimes I think we're supposed to fight. Some days I want her paying me attention, and some I want her out of my sight forever.

I feel stronger. Like maybe what was bothering me isn't as bad as I thought before and I can manage my emotions as long as I keep a healthy distance and keep doing whatever I want.

I made a sandwich in the kitchen earlier, didn't notice Momma sitting at the table until much later. She was sitting there with a half-empty beer falling over in her lap, and her eyes were leaking like she'd poured the drink right into them.

Had to wonder for a minute if she'd fallen asleep or died sitting up. It was intriguing.

"Sawyer, are you and your uncle getting along?" If cigarettes could speak, the husk in their voice would match hers. A raggedy voice.

"Fine," I said.

"Are y'all bonding?"

"Define bonding."

"Having fun?"

Define fun. I nodded.

I have no feelings about my uncle except for objective ones that any normal person would have. He's a bozo with a limited mind. And all the men Momma has chosen as good men have been bozos. I don't think Rod is the best person for a mentally ill person to be spending time with. I don't think Momma understands my condition. The doctor doesn't either.

"How's the doctor treating you?" she asked.

"He's fine."

"Just fine?"

"Just fine."

She was flicking her lighter incessantly and cursing it for running out of fluid. She asked me if the medicine was working. I didn't have the heart to tell her I'd crushed most of it and sprinkled it over a nest of hornets.

I don't want to not feel, and the medicine makes me not feel a thing.

Momma said, "I think you're in a good place to stop the talking."

I found that interesting. It's been four weeks of therapy and hundreds of weeks of bad parenting.

It's not just the treatment center that embarrassed Momma—it's having a kid in therapy at all. She's rushing to pretend I'm better when mostly I'm still the same person I was.

She is ashamed of herself, I think. Talks about moving. We never do. I think Momma secretly likes it here, hiding from everyone.

She's a waiter. Nice-enough job. She should make better dinners and give me more money on my birthday. She doesn't. She checked on me at Hapeville only to harass my crisis counselor about when I could leave. Threw a fit when Tom said I'd have to decide that for myself.

"We're gonna get you out of therapy." She went to the junk drawer and searched for something, not looking at me at all. "That sound good?"

Underneath the scissors, matches, and plasticware were the forms Tom sent me off with that advise "no proximity to guns, rope, extension cords, or anything that can be fashioned into a noose; a six-month treatment program with a therapist; and regular check-ins with a psychiatrist."

She located a match, slammed the drawer shut, lit a cigarette.

The trouble with my mother is she's too busy pretending problems don't exist to ever really fix them.

JAKE

After my date with Allister, my body feels featherlight and anxious.

I toss under the sheets at 11:59 p.m., desperate to hold on to the final dredges of the day's positivity and maintain this excitement. My brain is not made to hold on to hope for very long. My eyes are designed to capture the tragedies of total strangers. So when I'm happy, I only imagine how long it will take my balance beam of joy to run out and when I'll inevitably hit the ground.

My phone rings—the 12:00 a.m. ringtone. I press snooze.

I'm plagued by this fear, which is starting to feel certain: Sawyer will show up with a floating knife. He will murder me in my sleep and leave my sheets with a stain of me. I don't know if I'd prefer that, or for him to murder more strangers and lead me to witness them until my mind turns so gruesome, it detaches from all things positive and my body becomes a shell of trauma.

I lie in half darkness under the moonlight and wander toward sleep, wondering about anger and evil. Where it comes from, how it sustains itself beyond life.

I'd like to be happy and leave people alone. Why don't other people want the same thing?

The song wakes me up at 1:30. Snooze.

2:30. Snooze.

Fleeting projections. Wasps circling a head of blond hair with a bloody hole in the side. And that wraith card's warning to me: *You may become a victim of someone's misdirected vengeance.*

To take a gun into a school and start shooting . . . To kill randomly. Without calculation or care. Nothing reasonable. Only deranged. So why couldn't I be next? Why couldn't anyone?

The xylophones play at 3:15, when the moonlight seems the brightest it's been all night. It sneaks in through the slats, casting soft light on my walls.

It feels protective, like the sky is watching what happens here. Only four more hours before I have to be awake.

I press stop on the rest of my alarms and roll over, letting my arm dangle off the side of the bed.

Maybe just for tonight, he's given me a break.

There's some rest in my chest as I close my eyes. A noise whispers across the carpet under the bed, but I'm sure I imagined it—nothing is there but my paranoia.

And a hand taking hold of my wrist.

It yanks me off the mattress. My body shakes the floor. I'm being pulled under, and under. My chin punches the bed frame, stopping my momentum.

There's a demon under the bed. Pain is roaring up in my head, through my shoulder, and down the string of veins constricted in this grip. My bones creak in its fingers.

"Seeseeseeseesee." The whisper comes with laughter.

The carpet is ripping my knees apart. My palm is driving into the bed rails, my heart shooting fire through my bloodstream. There is something so angry about this tug-of-war.

"I'm sorry," I moan. *"Please."* I must be on punishment for something. If I can reason with it, maybe it will stop.

Sweat pushes down the hills of my body. The demon's nails tear into my wrist.

There's a cackling. *"HA HA HA HA HA!"*

How long have you been here? Living under my bed? I am so unaware. I never see what's happening right around me.

This fight is uneven, and the foe is some shape-shifting, invisible entity changing its method of harm. The hand is now a bracelet of barbed wire, tearing deeper and deeper . . . through my skin.

"HELP!" I shout into the house. "HELP ME!"

And then it lets go. All at once.

I pull my hand back and grab it, just to make sure it's still there. It is.

My back hits the wall. There's no blood. Thank God there is no blood, and no pain.

The cackling is gone. The chaos over. The moonlight still frames my room like a security spotlight, quiet and unfeeling, as if God saw everything that happened and simply did not care.

The demon returns.

Crawling up the corner of two walls across the room like a rabid squirrel. He's wearing a gray hoodie, with shoulder blades that are bent like they're trying to meet, arms curled like a raptor's, white hands the most human thing about him.

Forget that I'm here. Forget that I'm here. My thoughts are chemical explosions—compounds with no balance, only panic.

Of course he won't forget that I'm here. I am the reason that he's here, as a cockroach or spider, thoughtless, moving in directionless crawling patterns across the walls.

He skitters along the ceiling, pattering the walls, and stops where the light fixture swallows his head.

His body turns to face me and drops from the neck. He hangs there like a vulture with its neck snapped. The moon illuminates a pair of blue eyes glowing from inside the glass bulb. Wide, like they can see everything, and bright, like they're a source of light themselves. Somehow, still so dead inside.

I rush to the nightstand drawer, rip out a bottle of Axe, and push down the button so a cloud of mist bursts in between us. It shoots through the bottom of one of his legs.

Sawyer hisses and throws a fit with his arms and legs. His body drops through the floor.

The room is silent once he's gone, the lingering smell of musky deodorant spray the only proof anything ever happened.

Hours pass. I stay awake. The walls brighten with the sunrise. At 7:00 a.m. sharp I get a text.

ALLISTER: Pancakes or waffles?

I'm too sleepy and paranoid for this.

ME: Pancakes, I think.

HIM: You think?

ME: Depends?

HIM: Everything depends with you.
Is it never just a definitive choice? Lol.

I'm out of it. I know I should be laughing, but I'm too distracted.

Through my morning routine, I ponder a response and wonder if responses even matter. Two different boys have managed to take up residence so quickly in my life—one who appears to be a psycho killer, and one who . . .

Well, I don't know who Allister is. He seems nice, but what does he want? His kindness feels suspect.

I get dressed and go back downstairs, where I find Benji awake and staring at the TV, paralyzed by a headline:

Body of Missing Heritage Student Kieran Waters Found in a Ditch

An eighteen-year-old found dead in the middle of the Jefferson Nature Trail, in Heritage.

"Viewer discretion is advised," the anchor warns. "The images you are about to see may be disturbing to sensitive viewers."

I want to peel my eyes away, but I can't. A picture pops up of a white torso with no blood running through it. The body is naked—bare chest and abdomen, with the private area blurred. A husk of a body.

"We gotta go." Mom steps into the living room as she slips into her jacket.

She picks up the remote and freezes as the anchors return with a new headline:

Elusive Atlanta Serial Killer Suspected in New Homicide

Elusive is only half of the story. It's a demon terrorizing the town.

"What is going on?" Mom says, her tone soft and petrified.

She's speaking to no one in particular. She's posing the question to the world.

This is Sawyer Doon's latest victim. The kid went to Sawyer's school.

⁙

In the truck, I search the newest victim's name.

Kieran Waters Heritage brings up a bunch of pictures from Heritage High's current soccer team. The boy from the most recent report is in the pics. A redhead in a red jersey, with his arms wrapped around his teammates. Sawyer's second victim. Well, technically his eighth.

The questions keep unfolding about where he exists on the pendulum between life and death.

How did you put someone in the ground?

⁙

That night, I think about taking the car keys from Mom's purse. It's nearly midnight, and she's asleep. She'd probably never know. But even if I am exploring a more daring side of myself, I'm still not bold enough to take it that far. Besides, I can't drive.

So I swipe Mom's bottle of sleeping pills from the cabinet instead and drag my bike out from the garage, through the house, so the noise won't alert anyone.

Motion-sensored LED lights attached to the wheels illuminate the spokes with studs of color. A taillight attached to the back fires a glow into the darkness.

I keep myself to one side of the curb. Each car that zooms by thrashes me with a breeze, and I picture myself slammed into at an intersection, doomed to the death loop, bones breaking again and again.

The one-story houses and community churches peel into pieces of city. My GPS fires instructions through my earphones, and I fold into the suburbs, past the darkened windows of family businesses, eateries, the farmers market, the town hall screaming Southern tradition.

The school is nestled inside a residential area. Here the streetlamps make small pockets of light inside spreads of darkness. Avenues are ablaze with falling leaves.

The speed bumps become more and more dramatic as plastic yellow signs in the shape of kids appear by driveways and mailboxes. *SLOW!* they warn drivers.

Heritage is a school like any other school, with red bricks, a flagpole, car lanes, and bus lanes. I pedal down a crosswalk to reach the carpool lane and then breeze past a marquee sign— GOT A DATE FOR HOMECOMING? it asks. I dream of a world where I can answer yes to that question, but now is not the time.

One thing sets this school apart. I pull the brakes and jerk to a stop, catching myself with one foot against the ground when I see it.

Sawyer, charging the doors with a machine gun in his hand. He passes me with no acknowledgment.

It's not the real him. Just a phantom of him—a residual image from the death loop of a victim. He's a projection of the real thing, a smoky red outline, with lifeless eyes and no mind of its own. Like the falling javelin and the knife that kills Matteo.

I circle to the back of the building. There, facing a sports field and a line of classroom trailers, I put down the kickstand of my bike, pop two sleeping pills, and sit against the bricks of the building.

Best-case scenario: some friendly security guard finds me, wakes me up, asks a few questions, and lets me off the hook.

Worst-case: Racist Karen peeks out her window and calls the cops on the Black boy passed out in front of her local school.

I can hear their screaming even from out here.

Breathe . . . breathe . . . breathe . . .

I'm terrified, but I can't afford to listen to that voice inside me telling me to go home. And besides, home isn't safe anymore, and if I don't stop Sawyer Doon, it never will be.

Questions float through my mind as I drift into sleep.

Why did you do it?

What did you want?

What do you want?

⁘

I wake up lying down on a cold floor. A hard, shiny tile shrouded in a creeping fog of ecto-mist . . . the hallway of the dead school.

The mist is so thick only the top lockers are visible. It brought me inside Heritage's walls, like I thought it would. It's everywhere in here, like pollination season, bathing everything in an electro-magnetic glow. The walls stretch up and fade right into the open air, a black abyss, thick with clouds of ecto-mist. At the end of the hallway, the floor ends in a lethal drop off the third floor. Past that drop, a wall of murky clouds crackle with sparks of light connecting between telephone poles. It's all a giant storm cloud.

There's a phantom Sawyer dragging the barrel of his machine gun along the floor, banging the buttstock against the lockers. Bullet shells and dust penetrate the air. Books explode from the arms of a girl and flop open across the floor, their pages disintegrating like ashfall.

The Sawyers fade and reappear, are reborn and die. His maniacal tune reverbs through the school, amplified sixteen times—a stadium music box blowing out a deceptive melody.

"Come out, come out, wherever you arrrrre!"

He's in terrible flashes, supercuts, everywhere I look. The lights flicker to reveal him with the rifle stock pressed against a boy's cheek and dim to the sound of him kicking a classroom door open. There's a pandemonium of shrieking, lockers vibrating like thick sticks on snare drums.

A police siren blares, sending shock waves across the floor, turning the whole foundation into rippling water. The floor disappears from underneath me, and I plummet, slamming into the tiles beneath, head and joints exploding as if this were real life.

I'm on a solid bathroom floor, in between blue stall doors and white sinks, one of which is exploding from the pipes, shooting out water like a busted hydrant.

There's a boy in a button-down and slacks on the other side of that stream, rolling up his sweater sleeve and raising a needle to his elbow. He pauses to look at me. "Who are you?" He pushes the plunger into his skin and sucks in a huge gulp of air. His boots fold sideways underneath him, and he tips. The walls tip with him, throwing the whole room sideways like a cube.

I hit the floor on my back, and face up at a ceiling of stall doors, which are closed one moment but open the next, like a nest of bats sprouting from a slumber.

A boy's body falls out from a toilet, and he hits the floor beside me, hard.

The doors shriek on their hinges as I push myself up in the river of water, becoming pink from stall boy's blood. His eyes are open and staring at nothing. My clothes are soaking, a light bursting, sparks shooting across the endless fountain. I clamber for the exit, the dead boy's dissolving, sweeping starlight across the room.

The hallway is a spinning disk of lockers, like a funhouse

tube—a carnival thing I never had a desire to go through, since I knew it would make me as queasy as I am right now.

"I've seen enough."

The mist hisses *shhhhh*, like a living entity calling the shots. It somersaults me up through the ceiling and through another wall, where I'm greeted by a factory of noise.

POP! CRASH! CLINK! BOOM! Sink units. Cabinets with test tubes and vials. A rack for lab coats. A snap of flame. A cork popping off a test tube stand. A phantom hand floating above a flask. Explosions—*BSSHHH!* Freak accidents happening free of human involvement.

A rumble reaches me through the noise. A familiar rumble, because I hear it so often in my world.

It's . . . a phone vibrating, from a storage cabinet in the corner of the room. Tiles appear as I approach the doors—squares of pink and green, arriving for one footstep, departing for the next.

Is he behind this door? Waiting to shoot me?

Maybe I'm an idiot who took the bait, and this nightmare-scape, this long, anguished death loop, is where he ultimately meant to lead me . . .

My fingers curl around the cold silver handle, and I pull the door open.

There's someone in there, in the right side of the closet, who flinches when I open the door. A girl with olive skin and a pie-shaped face, bunched up with her knees to her chest and a phone sitting next to her.

I kneel to meet her. "Hi."

"Hi?"

Heavy eyeliner. A cartilage piercing and a moon necklace that sinks into her chest like an arc reactor. Straightened hair falls over one eye and her shoulders, lilting lightly like thin curtains. Some of the light from behind me reflects off her glasses and skin. Even though she died, she stayed closer to the Here than the After. She seems trapped in some state of being, both alive and dead.

"Who are you?" she asks.

"I'm Jake. You?"

"River."

"Hi. It's nice to find another . . . um . . . *aware* person in this nightmare school."

"I've never seen you before," River says. "Did you go to Heritage?"

"I'm actually a medium. I'm not even from here—I'm from DeKalb. Clark City."

"A medium?" She lowers her knees. There's a big spot of dark blood seeping through the front of her shirt. "So you're contacting me from the world of the living?"

"It's weird. I kind of just go where the mist takes me. Well, I came here on my own because I wanted to see it."

"Ah. The grand spectacle of the school where it happened."

River raises her arm, it seems, to push hair out of her face, but her hand is missing. Her forearm ends in a stub of exposed membrane, cauterized in a crust of twinkling light.

She scoots out of the closet, and I move back some to make room, checking behind me to make sure there's still floor. "How's it done, anyway? How do mediums cross worlds?"

"It's all still new to me. Shouldn't be, because I'm sixteen, but I spent my whole life until, like, two weeks ago trying to ignore it. Trying to run away. And then Sawyer showed up."

River flinches and then lets in a breath she doesn't let out.

"Here I was thinking his reign had ended in this school," she says. "I still hear him constantly. *Come out, come out, wherever you are.* Can barely tell if it's real or I'm imagining it. Same with everything else in this world." River turns back to her phone. In every spare moment, she seems obsessed with picking it up, but she has no hands. "They say when you're a ghost you're supposed to be able to reach the living. But I can't even reach my mom."

DMM! A locker slams.

"You lost your hands," I say.

"They didn't cross over with me, for some reason."

I pull my knees to my chest and look around at the holes in the floor, which sear orange at the edges, like the tops of volcanoes. "What happened in here with Sawyer? If you don't mind my asking."

It takes her a minute. Her lips dance on words, and when she speaks, it's a whisper. "He just went berserk. I didn't know he was violent until . . . I mean, you can't ever really expect it, can you? I used to watch him pick his nails off and eat them. Pull his hair out, leave it on the desk. I always thought *that kid is so fucking aggravated, that kid will snap, better be nice to him.* So I tried to be. I was coming from the bathroom when I heard the gunshots; everybody was running out of the room, but I thought it'd be smarter to hide. Hid in here thinking . . . I said hi to Sawyer even when other kids ignored him, so I thought he wouldn't shoot me . . . but then he did. Knocked my phone out of my hand so I couldn't send any messages first."

River looks like she's spent ages trying to find an answer to an answerless question.

"He's getting his power from his victims," I realize aloud.

"Is that what it is?"

"Maybe this is what he's challenging me to discover. And this is why he's following me everywhere. It's a game to see if I can save his next victims before he kills them. They must be kids he wanted to kill but didn't on his first killing spree."

River's eyebrows crease. "I always thought I'd live a short life, for some reason. But I didn't want any of my friends to."

I don't know how it's possible, but in the astral state I always feel completely in the nude. Like nothing is holding me down— not even my hoodie, which is clearly cloaking my upper half, and not my jeans, which are on my legs despite being somewhat swallowed by the atmosphere around them.

Sssssssssssss. Mist swims around the bones of my wrist and seeps into the lines of my hand, like glowing plankton. It lifts from my palm, first as a spiral, then a channel that extends toward River, caressing her like puppet strings, lifting her arm.

"What is this?" She's confused and intrigued. "An electro-magnetic Slinky?"

"Maybe dead world is pushing us to connect our energy."

"Why?"

The mist claws up to our chests and sinks inside us, pulling us together and into each other until we vortex into one, clashing with a crack in the elbows, a tremor in the lungs. Thermal light sprays across my mind, with sounds—a lawn mower, a barking dog. Visuals—a middle-aged Black man cutting the grass in his lounge shorts, a pit bull running to greet me in a lawn.

Then I open my eyes to the room, which looks different now— more complete, with columns of windows that show the sky. A whiteboard materializes, floating against the dulled white of the classroom wall. And then the door—a wooden panel.

This is trippy, River thinks. *As fuck.*

We rip the door open and launch into a stumble down the

endless hallway, where the floor falls off at the end. Our feet move, barely in sync. She says left when I say right, so it's all my body can do to stumble.

But we're moving toward the edge of the building, the ecto-mist creating a cryogenic chamber in my rib cage as I coordinate River's movements with mine. Her entire posture is different—her shoulders are more hunched, and her feet fall heavier. I adjust myself, shrinking my neck and refusing the use of my arms.

A stroke of lightning tears through the atmosphere outside, striking a tree, which tips like a falling titan. A whole grid of houses is being crushed by falling trees and telephone poles, and on the road, a bus is tipping over. It landslides over the sidewalk and hits a telephone pole.

At the end of the hallway I fall to my knees, cupping my fingers over the tile and concrete at the building's edge. My body below is like a distant speck on the sidewalk lining Heritage's wall. Sawyer—the real one, it seems, judging from his stillness—is standing over my body. His eyes are lifeless, his arms out like a scarecrow's. And I'm mirroring him, stretched across the wall like Jesus on the cross, a black vortex traveling from the gape of my mouth and into his as he drains me of life.

River and I break from the floor and end up floating in the middle of the air, the ecto-mist tearing through the dark clouds above us and casting its wind in a vortex that pulls us down to meet my physical self.

The mist rushes through me, like it's part of me, sinking in through the pores of my skin as I draw closer to myself and find my feet on the ground.

I pull a brick from the building and imagine it thicker until it densifies in my hand.

Throw it. It's a whisper, not from River's mind or my own, but from the mist itself.

I throw the brick, and it breaks across his head in a storm of dizzy ash.

He turns to face me, slowly, calmly. "You found me." It's like he was expecting me. His energy surrounds him in swaddles of red and black.

"Did you expect me not to?" My voice is layered—two voices at once.

His eyes are suspicious of something. "You're getting better at using this stuff."

"And you're uglier than you've ever been." River. That was definitely River's voice.

Sawyer lifts a whip and snaps it against the air. Mist flares down my arms like fire, forming a sword of blue energy. Sawyer thrashes the whip. I swing up and slice it, a spray of dusty light breaking both weapons.

He leaps toward the sky, to the top of the school, and I erupt after him, so high an aerial view of the building appears beneath—unfinished walls, floors in jagged edges, structure beams peeking through the roof. I pull myself down and hit the platform of tarmac, my weight sending a tremor across the roof, my feet sinking slightly through it.

Sawyer's waiting for me at the end of a gap into the hallway. His eye burns red, like a smashed cherry. Acne appears and then pops around his cheeks. His lips fade from white to blue to pink.

His eyes blacken, and he tears at his neck, ripping open the skin so that tendrils of red energy can crawl their way out. They tether red hands onto silky strings. Wraiths, coming toward me.

They seize my throat and lift me up, shrinking the school as

125

a black curtain falls over my eyes. Sawyer's aura calms. My legs kick for dear life, desperate to hold on to some semblance of my surroundings. But everything is blackening the farther up I go, like I'm drowning in the wrong direction.

NO. A voice erupts from the darkness. "NO."

Mist burns down the lengths of my arms, up my neck so it blinds me.

Kill him, it whispers. *Kill him.*

It's an order, not a suggestion. Not from River, or me, or any one voice. It's a chorus of them, in one rhythm, all saying the same thing. *Kill him, sssssssssissssss.*

I fall to the roof, landing like a dancer, a network of power coursing through my hands. I shoot him once in the chest, knocking him off balance. He runs forward, legs flying off the ground like a racehorse, and charges through me. I collapse in a fragile heap as River and Sawyer roll from my body, a tangle of grabbing hands and legs, barely there through the static of them.

Their momentum stops in the middle of the roof. River's on her butt, backing away, and he's rising above her, the gun trained on her forehead.

I shoot another ecto-blast, which hits his gun and sends it twirling from his hands. He turns to face me, and River finds her feet, connects her arms to his, then rips them out, stealing back her hands.

They fasten at the ends of her forearms, already balled into glowing fists. She throws a punch, and her hand knocks him off-kilter, disappearing through his face and returning to her wrist a moment later. She tackles him and lays into his face.

"AHHHHHHH!" she screams, anger roaring from her throat with her punches—punches hard enough to hear cracks forming in the matter of his being. Pieces of his face break off in red bouts of dust, disfiguring it.

Then he's a vanishing fume, tearing at the sleeves and legs and neck, an unconscious being melting like sugar in water through the roof.

River falls back on her feet and looks at her hands, her chest shaking with some essence of life—if not the breath humans breathe, then something even stronger. And she starts to float, back slightly bent, arms and legs waving like strips of a flag. Particles of light peel away from her feet and legs, and pieces of her travel like glittering doves through the darkness.

"What's going on?" The ecto-mist eats at her skate shoes, up her jeans, the fabric of her band shirt—tiny stars making homes for themselves in her skin and bones. Her hair burns white, each strand glowing hot. A snake of light fastens around her head like a crown.

"I think you're . . . passing on to the After?" With one hand in front of my forehead, I watch her face break in a constellated crack and burst into mist. Her body rushes through the darkness and lifts me in its electric wind. My sweater and shirt billow like the chutes of a sailboat as the glowing stream throws me to the tarmac and then rips like a determined fish through the darkness beyond.

I watch it soar and then vanish into the dark, beyond where my eyes can reach.

Was Sawyer's defeat tied to River's death loop? If so, her passing on would mean we've beaten him. But it doesn't seem that way. I could swear I saw him moving away on purpose, like his energy had run out and he needed to restore it.

The wind pulls me backward, and my eyes spring open to the real world, where I had passed out on a square of asphalt. I squeeze my eyes shut against the security light above me.

"Fuck—" A headache breaks in my skull as I make sense of

the school building. My phone is in my hand, my thumb jittering over a new text message. Keysmash is all that's in the box.

My face is bleeding. Yellow bruises around my wrists. Elbows ripped open to their cherry-red states. Blood leaking through my jeans at the knees. Cuts all over my knuckles, like I fist-fought a stone. I plant my hands on the leather of my shoes and then erupt like a strike of lightning from the pavement.

"Ouch." My voice is a whimper.

I find my bike against the wall, and I roll it onto the pavement. "Never again. Never."

Is it over? I wonder as I swing my leg over the seat and push off. My feet dip and rise as the wheels turn, taking me down the carpool lane, through the phantom Sawyer. His clouds pass like gun smoke over my shoulders.

Are you coming back?

Onward to the crosswalk and out of the school zone, my safety is compounded by dread as behind me, a bus keeps crashing and crashing.

JAKE

The Heritage hellscape makes a daze of my Saturday morning. I make an egg sandwich, take one bite, and leave it in the fridge. I sweep dust off the extremely white quartz countertop. My weight feels ugly—heavy and hunched over, like my spine is trying to turn me into a wood bug. My stomach hates food.

Sawyer is getting all that energy from his school for his strikes. How long will I have to fight him? Ordinary ghosts exhaust their fear, panic, and grief by flickering lights, flipping chairs, rapping on windows. They're starved for attention. Then they get it, and they're done.

Sawyer . . . he's never gonna be done until I'm dead, is he?

River passed on. Now she must be part of all this hissing dust eclipsing the sunlight between the window and kitchen. Something about confronting Sawyer, about beating him the second time, propelled her into the afterlife. But that doesn't mean Sawyer is gone—it just means his memory in her life has no power to trap her anymore.

That was never my fight. Sawyer's still waiting for me. I can feel it. Still standing in the shadow of some distressed teen who met his final hour under the barrel of his gun, sucking a piece of them into his final form.

❖

School on Monday is a bleak blur—everything dull and less important than usual. The locker room at PE is a maelstrom of hooting and thrashing, the smell of half-naked white boy creating a stench.

I change in the bathroom, in a nook away from the main area. My knees are stinging, my fingers weak around the band of my sweatpants as I pull them up. There are gashes on my hands where it looks like a paring knife peeled back the skin. Bruises form valleys in my wrist. I should know when all this damage occurred, but I can't even remember.

After dressing, I hug the wall, still feeling this extreme sense of post-astral jet lag. There are whispers in my mind and the image of Sawyer pointing a gun in my face. I'm half-afraid everything will start tipping and throw me on my head.

BANG! The door shakes. "We saw you go in there, Jake."

Chad. A rumble of laughter spurs him on—he always has a bigger audience than he deserves.

I check the sliding bolt to make sure it's really locked, because if it opens, I'm doomed. Chad must hate my whole family now that my brother hooked up with his girlfriend. But he hated me even before that, I think for a worse reason. I think it's because I'm Black.

"What's wrong, Jake? Scared to change with all the other boys? Afraid someone will see your micro-dick?"

The laughter is loud, and the sound makes me nauseous—it's so ugly to make fun of other people, but somehow it brings them so much joy.

I don't say anything. I just close my eyes and breathe.

He bangs on the door again, so hard the hinges squeak. He whispers the next part through the door crack. "I'mma start calling you Little-Dick Jake. Your whole family probably has little dicks."

"I'm not interested in a date with you, Chad." My voice is weak.

People laugh at my comeback, but it's not as enthusiastic. It's awkward, and my attack wasn't strong enough or believable enough, which is why I usually don't say anything. I don't have muscles or play sports, and in a fight with him I'd end up with a mutilated face and no support. Grady's out there too and saying nothing. I guess I let our friendship down.

Chad is quiet. I've won this round.

I sit on the toilet and wait for everyone to leave before coming out into the silent locker room. I'm going to projectile vomit all over the tiles if I don't get my mood in order.

Bullies in the real world need to be handled too. I wish my power could amount to more than just death and soul projection. If I can't even handle life, how the hell am I gonna banish Sawyer?

When I get outside, everyone's already running the warm-up laps. I hug my sweatshirt, press my beanie to my ears.

Don't pass out or throw up. One foot after the next.

The ecto-mist is busy today. Crackling like static in the tennis court fence, spiraling up the yokes of St. Clair's belfry.

Is all of that mine to use and control?

Two people arrive on either side of me. Fiona and Allister. Allister, whose St. Clair Saber Cats sweatshirt is so tight against his arms I want him to put me in a headlock.

"You know, you don't always have to run by yourself, Jake," Fiona says.

She runs kind of like a scavenger, small and determined, her whole body twisting in the motion. Allister runs like an Olympic triathlete, his torso upright and his fists bunched up by his chest.

"Do you two know each other?" I ask.

"We bonded over our love for *Fruits Basket* in trig," Allister says. "Aaaaand at some point we realized we had a mutual friend."

"Who, me?"

"Duh, you," Fiona says.

"Where's Amanda?"

"Somewhere else. I'm not even sure we're friends anymore."

"What happened?" Allister and I ask in unison.

"Jinx!" he says. "You owe me . . . um . . ." He looks at Fiona and cancels his thought.

What were you going to say? I wonder. *What do I owe you?*

Fiona squeezes her ponytail tighter so it jostles against the back of her neck. "Nothing happened. She's just judgmental. All she wants to do is talk about what people *shouldn't* be doing."

"Sounds like pure hell," Allister says.

Allister had gotten into his sports clothes without visiting the locker room at all. Maybe he changes in private bathroom stalls, like me, because he's uncomfortable too.

"Anyway," Fiona says. "Do you guys want to go on an after-school venture on my favorite nature trail?"

"What does an after-school venture entail? Walking?" I ask.

"Could be anything we want it to be, as long as it's spontaneous. Planning ruins the purpose."

"Sure thing." Allister starts snapping his fingers with glee. "We were just talking the other day about how Jake could afford to get out of the house more."

"I don't remember that at all?" I mean, not in those words.

"Did you forget about our date already?"

"No! Of course not, but we never talked ab—" *Wait a minute.* "Date? Is that what that was?"

"Anyway, Fiona, like I was saying." Allister swerves back into the conversation. "You can't hold yourself back or just be there for someone else's benefit."

Smooth, man . . . The freezing air adds a cold blue tint to his lips. He's beautiful.

Fiona reverses into a backward jog to stare us down. "Quick question. Are y'all by any chance dating?"

"NO!" we both scream.

"Okay." She looks incredulous as she pivots. "Just a question."

Allister and I might be a little too close. Our arms are brushing against each other and our feet hitting the track at the same time.

"Yo, Jake!" It's Grady, running up behind me.

Oh, brother.

Grady was tying his shoes on the bench when I walked into the locker room, and he said nothing when they were clowning me. Fiona would stick up for me if she were there. Allister would too.

What's the point of having friends if they're just gonna keep quiet when you need them to have your back? If they're just gonna give you the cold shoulder because you didn't elevate their social clout? Now he wants my attention. And he's not gonna get it.

Allister looks behind him. "Uh, Jake? Your friend is calling you."

"I know." And I'm ignoring him. "I'm down for an after-school venture."

"Yes!"

Fiona pumps her fist, and I'm excited for three seconds before the crushing realization that Sawyer may tag along takes over me.

What are you doing now? I wonder as we pass the castle of my school and loop around the goalpost. *Who are you targeting next?*

I haven't slept in days because I'm too fucking paranoid, and I can't even talk about it. If I do, the only true friends I've ever made will think I'm crazy.

✛

Six hours and a lunch date later, Fiona, Allister, and I meet again in the parking lot and head to the Sunwood Nature Trail, five blocks from campus. It's nice being out here. Hiking isn't so bad when it's with people you like.

Allister ambles up the steps of a gazebo, swinging his arms and twirling. Fiona follows, so I do too, into the gazebo, which forms a platform in the forest and provides a 360 of it.

There's a death loop happening about a hundred yards away. A man digging a hole. There's a giant garbage bag next to him. He's taking a break, leaning on his shovel, wiping sweat off his forehead.

Fiona sits and opens her bag. Then she takes out a smaller bag, of something green. Weed?

Back to the man. He's picking up the bag. There's hair spilling out of the top. A wife, probably.

"Your brother gives me the *best* stuff," Fiona says.

I cringe. It's an embarrassing reminder my brother is St. Clair's most renowned and trusted weed dealer.

Allister's up and down in his seat. "Light me up, light me up."

"Are y'all really about to smoke right here?"

"Of course we are," Allister says. "This has been the worst day ever. Mr. Shaw nearly gave me an aneurysm in chemistry. Asked me for the formula for ammonium. Who the fuck knows that? I hate when teachers ask you things just to embarrass you. I deserve this treat."

"What if someone comes?" I ask.

"We are *not* offering them any," Fiona says, and they both

134

laugh as she rolls a joint. I look frantically around me. No one's out here except for the ghost man, who's almost finished his hole.

If Sawyer really is responsible for the death of Kieran Waters, it means he killed him and brought his body out to hide it. That means he's upgraded his abilities since Matteo's murder, which happened sloppily and ended right there, in his bedroom.

Even a living person has trouble moving a body. But Sawyer seemed to do it without a problem. Maybe he hangs out at Heritage High because it's his source of power. Maybe that power comes from his memory of the shooting.

How can I remove his memory?

Fiona's handing me the joint.

"I'm second?"

"Hit it slow," she says.

I bring the j to my lips, inhale, and start coughing. And coughing. My throat feels like someone threw ashes into it. "Is it supposed to feel like you're—um—*dying*?"

Allister takes it off my hands. "Try not to take too much at one time, friend." He leans back, pulls, and then blows his smoke into the frigid air, with no trace of respiratory struggle.

"Sorry." I look down at the tassels on my loafers. "I know I'm not cool like my brother."

"Please." Fiona waves a hand. "You're actually very cool. Just in a different, kind of brooding to yourself, zoned-out sort of way. More than one way to be cool."

"Our parents always let us do our own thing. Probably why I came out so different."

I'm high already. The person burying that body has blurred into the fog, and the shovels of dirt look more like dust. The ghost is disappearing piece by piece. The dead world is vanishing, the real world brightening, birdsong traveling farther under the canopy, the orange-pink sky like a delicious sorbet above.

Fiona pulls a pair of climbing gloves from her backpack. "If you all will excuse me, there's a giant tree over there begging me to climb it."

"You are *not* about to climb a tree," Allister says, laughing.

She steps off the gazebo with a coy smile, eyes slightly red and half-closed. "Feel free to join me."

"I'm good."

"Please be careful," I say as she runs off into the trees.

I'm really glad to have a moment alone with Allister. I feel like I can trust him.

"If I told you something crazy, would you judge me?" I ask.

"Depends how crazy," he says.

"Do you believe in ghosts?"

"Absolutely." He looks at me. "Can you see them?"

I'm silent. That's his answer. I might have denied it, but I'm taken aback by how fast he got there.

He smiles. "That's awesome. Wish I could do that."

"Um . . . it's not always awesome. It's usually pretty scary."

"So that's why you're so quiet? You're distracted by the dead."

"I . . . I guess so. Among other reasons, probably. I don't know why I'm so quiet, exactly."

Not everyone thinks I'm crazy, even if my family does. There's a wave of relief coming over me. I've never heard it taken so seriously except with Ms. Josette and my online medium community. Growing up, I always had to explain myself and beg people to believe me, so I stopped telling people at all.

"What's going on?" Allister asks. "Why do you look so troubled?"

"My neighbor was killed two and a half weeks ago." I'm

unable to stop myself. "Matteo Mooney. It's been on my mind a lot because everyone thinks it's a serial killer, but it's a ghost that took him. A vengeful one who wants to kill more people. And I've done what I can to get rid of him, but I keep thinking it's not over . . . He's still out there, and he's planning to attack me again. I don't know. I know it sounds crazy."

His face is genuinely somber. He can feel the fear too. "It doesn't sound crazy. Sounds scary, though. Any leads on who it could be?"

I hesitate. It feels wrong to say his name. Like it's cursed. And I'm afraid Allister will shun me like Benji did.

"It's okay, Jake," he says. "You can tell me."

"S-S-S—" I stutter on the sound of it. "Sawyer Doon. From the Heritage High shooting." It deflates from my mouth sooner than I'm ready.

Fiona returns before I can say much more, jumping into the middle of the circle, catching her breath. "What'd I miss?"

"Nothing," I answer, but at the same time, Allister says, "Nothing—just Jake revealing he can see the dead."

Wow. "Really, Allister? *Why?*"

"What? It's cool and Fiona's cool."

She doesn't look surprised. Only intrigued. "My grandmother saw spirits too."

"Really?"

"Yeah. They low-key haunted us growing up, but she was able to tell which ones were good and which ones were bad, so it was never that scary."

I always forget ghosts have an entire lore. I'm not exactly overflowing with other medium friends, but even a regular person can feel a haunt in the room, a weird lilt in the wind, a noise.

Seeing the darkness so vividly always tricks me into thinking I'm the only one who can see it at all.

On our way to the parking lot, I spill to Fiona and Allister about astral projection—how I don't understand how best to control it yet, but it keeps happening and will inevitably happen again. I tell them about the blood on the walls, the writing in my book, the connection to the so-called killer on the news, whose crimes are both mysteriously tied to former Heritage students.

How anyone who attended that school and walked out alive could be in danger of being killed.

"Yeah," Allister says as we enter the arena of trees where his car is parked. "We're definitely gonna have to kill this fucker." He pulls a laptop out of a bag and sits on the trunk.

We join him on either side, legs dangling.

"Let's see if we can find out a little more about this family," Allister says. "Sorry, Dad. I don't think you expected me to be breaking into the courthouse record system when you taught me about cybersecurity, but lessons always lead to more lessons." His fingers type away at the keys.

"So, the address in the book led you to Matteo's house," Fiona says. "That must mean Sawyer wants you on the trail of his crimes. Like, he's trying to lure you into some twisted game."

"He wants me dead at the end of it," I say. "But alive, in a sense. He wants me to see everything that's happening until I'm so traumatized, I barely have the resolve to fight back. And then, when my body is so weak and my mind so full of horrific shit that I don't even want to get out of bed anymore, that's when he'll jump in."

Allister types hard on his keyboard, and I lean on the trunk to watch the screen, catching a dizzying whiff of lotion or cologne—something sweet. He's acting like he has only one minute to type a code that will save the universe.

"Aaaand . . . voilà!" he chirps. "There's a Joy Doon in Heritage. Does that sound right? Voter registration info shows a Morning-side Drive address."

"You found her that freaking fast?"

The list of names on his screen appear in green type, like a matrix of codes. There are only three of them—Joy, Mary, and Steve. Not a lot of people named Doon in the city of Heritage.

In Sawyer's house there might be some essay he wrote, or cards that contain info about his weaknesses or motivations, or the kinds of energy he feeds from, specifically, so I can deprive him of it.

Hands in my hoodie, I start to pace between them, remembering the tools Sawyer used to fight me—whips, and then hands—horrifying wraiths conjured in midair, seeming to come straight out of him. They took me by surprise, maybe because they were so fleeting and haunting. If I had access to all of his memories, I would know his weapons of choice and the objects of fear I could use to defeat him.

"A journal. Maybe Sawyer had a journal."

Allister raises his eyebrows, and I know that I'm onto something. "You think they'd keep that in the house?"

"Maybe. If it wasn't too disturbing. Maybe as a trinket to remember him by."

"You'd have to search it." Fiona's leaning on the back door, eating sour straws and writing something down in her notebook. "Which is possible with a story and a distraction. You'd need someone who looks like she means no harm and who can spin a convincing story."

Allister's still doing research. "Looks like Joy Doon is involved with the Found Project. A charity that benefits homeless LGBTQ youth."

"I've heard of them!" Fiona says. "They help homeless queer kids. So we say we're there to advocate for housing programs in Atlanta."

Allister closes his laptop. "Sounds good to me!"

"Wait a minute." I'm feeling queasy about the whole thing. "Are we . . . actually doing this?"

⌖

Minutes later, we're driving to Sawyer's house. The windows are down, but I can't breathe.

I'm holding on to the passenger door handle. "So . . . we're breaking into someone's house. Okay. Cool. Casual."

"We're not breaking in," Fiona corrects me from the back seat. "We're *door-knocking*."

"Okay, door-knocking. Who lets door knockers into their house these days?"

"Trust me. I'll get into the house and text y'all when the coast is clear to come in through the back. Just be as stealthy as you can."

"And if it's not there? I mean, what are the odds I find his diary?"

"Then it's not," Fiona says. "And we leave, having gone on a satisfying after-school venture."

"So you meant 'robbery' when you said that."

"It's no fun if you know what you mean when you say it!"

The sun's just setting when the GPS lands us on a strip of dirt road. There's barely a path. The trees are so thick their branches scrape against the windshield. The wheels snap branches as the car rolls over them.

"Okay, house in the forest? I'm not driving over this," Allister says, stopping the car.

140

In the distance, through the trees, I see pieces of a shed . . . behind it, a porch. It's nearly hidden from view, but it's the only house out here. That must be it. We're parked enough out of the way that the car is obscured by underbrush, a few yards away from the entrance.

My stomach is boiling. "There's no fucking way she'll believe door knockers who came out of nowhere to approach her forest home."

"Oh, God." Allister pinches the bridge of his nose. "Let Fiona handle it, Jake! We'll wait in the car. Two Black boys barging in at once is what will stretch the credibility for Ms. Karen Doon."

Fiona seems unfazed by the fact that we're in the forest— actually, she seems more excited. She rips out a sheet of notebook paper and writes SORRY in red Sharpie. She gets out and slaps it over the license plate.

Allister watches her through the back windshield. "Wow. She's thorough."

"Hi, Mrs. Doon?" Fiona rehearses in the window. She pokes her head through the car door. "Be ready to speed off at a moment's notice."

And off she goes to ring the bell on the front porch. I sink down in my seat and pull my shirt half over my face. She glances back and gives us a wink.

"Look at her," Allister says. "Using her privilege for good. Ain't that something?"

"Yeah. This is not gonna work."

"We really need to work on your pessimism."

She rings the doorbell again when no one comes.

Allister asks, "How do you feel about her, anyway? Fiona. Do you like her?"

"Of course I do."

"No, I mean do you *like* her."

"Oh . . . no. Haven't thought about her that way. We're just friends."

A blond lady opens the door. It must be Sawyer's mom. She's in a denim shirt buttoned all the way up. I can't make out her features from way back here, but her face looks tired, her cheeks hungry.

I've never heard anyone talk about what happened to Sawyer's family. It's almost like they were just accepted as part of the mistake.

Fiona starts talking. And they continue talking. A full minute passes, with Allister and me holding our breath, watching through the branches that hang over the windshield. I'm half expecting the woman to see us in the car. How concealed are we, really?

But her attention doesn't leave Fiona.

"It's working," Allister whispers.

There's sweat leaking from my armpits. I want to hold his hand to make it all easier, but it's way too soon.

Fiona walks into the house, and the door closes behind them. I get out of the car and hop in the front seat, just to be next to Allister. I'm relieved Fiona got past the porch, but terrified. This means I'll have to actually break in and find Sawyer's diary now.

"See? That wasn't so hard, was it?" Allister asks.

"Okay, but it's not over. Not even close. It's just getting started. Her kid was obviously a gun enthusiast—what if she is too? What if she shoots me?"

"Do you want me to go instead?"

"No. Of course not. I can't put you in danger like that."

"Okay, in that case, if you're risking your life today, I need you to know something. Now that you've confessed your secret . . . I have one too."

I've never seen him look so serious, and I'm worried what will come next will heap another layer of anxiety on what I'm already feeling.

He waits a few seconds, but it's still not long enough. "I . . . have kind of a crush on you."

Wait a minute. *What?* Did I just hear that? Am I still high?

His eyes look weaker than I've ever seen them.

"Why?" I ask.

He laughs awkwardly. "Why not? You're super sweet . . . and you're a psychic. What else is there?"

I feel like an idiot. Leave it to me to ruin a moment that's supposed to be romantic. But he couldn't have picked a worse time to drop that on me.

"I get it if you're straight," he says. "And hopefully you're not homophobic and this won't ruin our short friendship, because I like it for what it is so far. But I just wanted to put it out there."

"No, not at all. Neither of those things. I mean . . . I just didn't expect it."

I like you too, I want to say. *But you're attractive . . . witty . . . funny . . . and I'm just Jake.*

More moments pass without a text from Fiona, and I'm getting worried.

"Hey." Allister brings my attention back to him. I expect anger or impatience, but his eyes are still safe. "You don't have to answer right away. I don't mean to put you on the spot. I'm just the kind of person who lets people know. Life's too short to hold it in."

I love that he says what he feels, and I want that so badly for myself, because here, in his car, would be a perfect spot to kiss him.

But Allister doesn't get that seeing ghosts is not always a cool thing. Sometimes it's a scary thing.

Sawyer leaked that video of Benji to the internet to drive a wedge between Benji and me. I don't always see him, and I don't know how he does it, but he follows me everywhere. And he'd try to hurt Allister if he saw me get close to him.

Allister said I didn't have to answer, but he's disappointed. The air was sprinkled with a soft pink glow, but now it's melting into a sad blue. His eyes trail outside the window at the falling leaves. His fingers tap the center console.

The silence is begging me to say something, but I . . . I . . .

A text beeps on my phone, reminding me why we're here. Allister leans over and reads it with me. *Back window, window cracked, NO SCREEN. Books on shelves and in closet. Tiptoe! Keep door closed! You have 5 minutes!*

I imagine her telling Sawyer's mom she needed to go to the bathroom and then taking it upon herself to explore other rooms in the meantime. What a genius. But five minutes is not long at all.

I start to jump out of the car and then hear, "Wait." Allister pops open the glove compartment and pulls out a pair of gloves, which look like they're for working out. "Wear these. That way, if they call the police, my fingerprints will be on the stuff instead."

"Allister—please."

"Jake—relax. There's no fingerprints on gloves. It was a joke. Just wear them."

"Oh . . . ha."

I slip on the gloves in a hurry. How much time do I have? Not much at all. Probably, like, four minutes and thirty seconds at this point.

I get out, close the door gently behind me, and break into a rapid tiptoe through the trees, toward the shed. I pull the hood of my sweatshirt over my head. The leaves tumbling off trees are red too, so I'll appear like an apparition among them, somewhat blending in.

Sticks and leaves crunch under my feet. The shed looked closer to the house from way back here. It's on its own, farther from the house than I'd expect any shed to be.

There's a ghost man and phantom deer behind it. The ghost man is a hunter, slinging his rifle over his back—he's got a fresh kill. Or so he thought. The deer, presumed dead, bucks its head, sticking its antlers through the hunter's chest. Both burst into light.

The trees form a body of snapped springs and broken nerves, and through this network I loop around to Sawyer's house as the depths of the forest pull me toward them, challenging me to keep running.

Maybe I could wind through these trees and just get lost. Let my feet take me somewhere new.

A burst of wind sweeps up a tornado of leaves in front of me. In the dust crinkle particles of electric blue. Ecto-mist. The storm doesn't calm and stands as a giant before me, like the universe has built an unbreakable barrier.

So I turn around. Take a right. And hustle past empty beer bottles, a rusty old tractor, and thorny bushes that pull at the bottoms of my jeans, under a hornet's nest growing from a branch like an infected lymph.

The sight of Sawyer's house turns my stomach. Puke green with a low roof weighed down by its moisture, seemingly built for one or two people.

I run for the house as quietly as possible, lift the cracked window, and climb through. My sneaker creaks against the floorboard. This room . . . is it a room? Or is it a dungeon of shoes, clothes, paintings, and pill bottles? Also . . . dirty dishes, cigarettes, and beer.

Gross . . . I can see why someone who grew up here would go crazy.

A fan whirs so fast on the ceiling it's rattling back and forth. A display of flowers and sympathy cards sits on a bookshelf. In the middle there's a picture of Sawyer smiling huge. On the shelves there are some paperbacks—*A Grief Observed, Living in a Gray World.*

But I want the closet . . . She said to search the closet . . .

I tiptoe closer to the cracked-open closet. Fiona's rehearsed laughter comes muffled from the living room. Sawyer's mom talking back. The floor creaks under my feet again.

"Fuck," I whisper.

A text from Fiona: *Running out of things to talk about. Let me know when you've looked.*

In the closet, there's a medium-sized box on the upper shelf and a mountain of clothes in between. There may be a hamper beneath them. If so, I can't see it. No way to move all these clothes. So I step on the pile and start climbing.

I reach up and feel under the box. Heavy.

I text Fiona, *please make some noise.*

First, the volume of her voice goes up, and then I hear glass crashing.

"I'm *so sorry!*"

Because I guess we're fucking up the whole house, I yank the box as hard as I can and tumble backward. I hit the floor on my back, with a pile of stuff avalanching on top of me, hitting me and the floor. I turn over, ignoring the pain in my forehead, and go through the items. Gift wrap? A wrench? A dead bouquet of flowers. Novels, and . . .

A breeze rushes through the open window, drawing in a blue dust, which whips back the cover of a journal, flips the pages, and closes it the opposite way.

"Thank you, ecto-mist," I whisper as I swipe up the book.

Inside, it reads: PROPERTY OF SAWYER. DO NOT READ.

"Oh, I'm definitely gonna read this, you little bitch."

My phone vibrates, and it triggers me. A text from Fiona on the screen: *GET OUT NOW.*

The door swings open, and a person walks in. A girl with Sawyer's hooked nose, pale skin, and blond hair. She stops dead when she sees me. We both freeze.

"Oh, hi!" I chirp. "I'm the organizer. I'm helping your mom get organized."

God, that was awful.

Face twisted with disgust, she lunges from the room, screaming, "MOMMAAAAAA!"

"Fuck." I pace around the items of the box. Do I try to make it look like I wasn't here?

I pick up the box, but it tumbles over, spitting out tapes and books and candles. The candles are labeled **WILDERNESS RESORT** and **WET WOOD**. The tapes are labeled **SAWYER'S FIFTEENTH** and **ANNIE—PROM**.

I tuck the journal in my jeans and dash across the room as a voice shrieks down the hallway. "MOMMA, CALL THE POLICE!"

The book falls out as I lift my leg to the windowsill. I dive for it, sweep it up, and launch out, landing in the muddy grass, journal pressed to my chest.

I take off like a running back into the trees and past the porch, where Fiona flies out the front door.

Allister's car is hidden, so I can't see him, but all of our lives are in danger. As I run, the mist lifts me, pushing me faster than

I thought possible, grazing my toes on just the tips of leaves until I'm crashing into the Hyundai, throwing myself into the back seat. Fiona bolts in like a torpedo behind me.

"DRIVE!" I scream at Allister, who's fiddling with the keys.

"Oh, shit." He sticks the key in, thrusts the gearshift forward, and floors it backward through the woods.

Sawyer's mom comes running down the front steps, holding a handgun. "Hey!"

Allister whips the car in a circle, narrowly avoiding a tree.

We roll over a hill as the lady fires the gun. BANG!

"AAAAAAHHHHH!" Fiona screams, diving to the floor.

I turn back around so the mom's gun is right in line with my eyes. If she shoots, she might break the windshield and kill me. Allister pushes forward, and I remember the license plate covered with Fiona's sign—SORRY.

Ms. Doon lowers the gun and lets us drive away, watching with somber indifference as Allister swerves through the trees, and we lose the house.

When we're back on the street, Fiona plunks down in the seat and curls up, laughing, her hair wild and loose around her. "What a RUSH! WHAT A RUSH!"

Allister's shaking his head. "Y'all are crazy. CRAZY. I'm finding new friends, okay? I swear to God."

I'm smiling and clutching the book. I got the journal. I one-upped Sawyer Doon.

Allister checks his mirrors and floors it down the street, leaving a cloud of exhaust in our wake.

JAKE

Read it," they're both telling me as we zoom off. "Read it out loud."

I stammer through my answer. "I should . . . um . . . I should read it alone first."

I'm glad I had help in retrieving it, but I don't want to give my friends more than they can handle all at once. And I know whatever's in here will be horrifying.

When we make it to my house, Allister gets out and walks me to my door. "Sorry if I made you feel uncomfortable today," he says.

"It's okay. It's nothing compared to . . . everything else."

"I know, but let me know if you need anything. Really. Even as a friend."

He steps off my porch like each step carries the weight of the world. My heart feels just as heavy watching him go down my driveway.

I run upstairs, fall on my bed, open the book, and read.

And read, about his mother.

And read, about his psychiatrist, and his sister, and his uncle.

I can hardly stomach the words from the mind of this kid. Well, deranged ghost. Dead stalker who once was a human trying to survive home and school, just like me. Not just a spirit show-ing up at random and leaving, but a full-fledged human who was here once, trying to navigate his life, just like me.

Just like me . . .

Just like me . . .

I fling the diary under my bed and curl up for a nap under the last escaping bit of daylight. I should wake up soon enough to stay awake all night.

Just like me.

He's in my nightmare, chasing me down the hallways of St. Clair. The lights flicker, and the gun goes off like a piledriver. It wakes me up, soaked in sweat, with an aching chest.

The sheets are wet, so I strip them, toss them in the wash, and rest my palms on the machine as the cycle starts.

Allister's words come back to me in a flash—*I have kind of a crush on you.*

That's sweet. Really exciting. Words like that are supposed to make me feel good. Instead, they just feel hard to believe. I'm not convinced they weren't part of some dream. But if he really does like me, and I like him back, that means normal social inter-action is just happening in a non-chaotic way in my life. I don't remember becoming worthy of something so nice.

I get in the shower and scrub off the stench of sweat in luke-warm water. The water escapes down the drain, and I wish I could go with it. *I have no idea how I'll ever tell anyone that I'm gay.*

I couldn't hold hands and walk around school with Allister like normal couples do, because everybody would judge us harder than they judge white gay boys. White gay boys can be gay because gay is all they are. Allister and I . . . we're Black *and* gay, and being both would put targets on our heads. No kissing in public, or at home. His house or hidden in public would be the only options.

There's no way that Allister Burroughs, light as the wind, would want to hide his lover from the world.

If I take things any further with Allister, I'll put him in Sawyer's line of fire.

Sawyer will just stop the happiness. The happier I get, the further he'll go to destroy it. That's all he ever wants to do.

"You have a beautiful body, Jake."

My eyes burn from the foaming chemicals of my shampoo. Through the rivulets of clear shower curtain, a pair of blue eyes is watching from the other side.

Sawyer wraps his hand around the curtain and yanks it back.

His jaw drops open; his eyes fill with black. A vortex forms between my face and his as he pulls a gritty indigo dust into the cavities of his face.

I break free and crumple into the wall, knee banging the shower knob. Climbing over the tub, I crank it down and crash through his body. The towel rack hits the palm of my hand as tufts of smoke—pale blond, gray-black—explode around me. The essence of Sawyer rips apart and pieces itself back together in the shape of a hand around my wrist. The hand yanks down.

SNAP! My wrist bones crack as the towel rack rips off the wall, plaster hanging on to its ends. I snatch the towel off the collapsing rod and throw it around my waist, stumbling toward the mirror. The sink vanity catches me, and I throw my head up and find myself alone. I know he's behind me, but my reflection doesn't. I can only feel him—a tickle at the back of my neck, a crinkle down my spine, like the tip of a finger tracing my body.

"I see you've made new friends." It's only his voice now, and his breath is like a blizzard on the back of my ear. "I wanted some once, but that dream died long before me."

He knows I like Allister, I realize in a panic.

"People. Aren't. Good."

He could make him his next victim.

"People. Are. Bad."

Does he know I took the journal?

It's possible he doesn't. More possible he does.

I have to escape the bathroom and hide the journal in a better place—he'll only get more violent if he knows what we did.

He pushes me into the sink, and I hit above the hips. He sinks his hand through mine. And in the mirror, my skin brightens until it's two shades paler than chestnut, and the brown irises of my eyes are wrapped in a cold blue. I smile against my will and find a snaggletooth in my mouth, an uncharacteristic yellow grime on my teeth.

A mental picture—Allister naked in front of me, his arms, wrists, and ankles wrapped in snaking ivy.

That thought . . . it wasn't mine. Was it?

Pretty boy snaking with the spades of dark green flowers. It's Sawyer's voice in my head—a dark country melody. *Pretty boy husk, pretty boy dust.*

I lean over the sink, gag, and spit. I come back up to face myself—my half-white, half-Black self. There is a black thing moving in my ear.

It's . . . a skinny, jointed fiber, like a piece of string. I drag it out of my ear canal. At the same time, hair follicles lengthen on my head, my curls straightening like springs pulled to the max, until my hair is falling in front of my face in drapes of straight black.

And the fiber stretches ever longer from my earlobe.

No, not a fiber. A leg. Two legs, creeping out of my ear cavity and catching my upper ear. A spider. Bulbous and brown with black patterns, wrenching itself out of my listening hole.

Blood trickles down my jawline as the spider crawls up the side of my face and nestles in my hair. I slap at my head and feel nothing but my head. Hair still short, despite what it looks like in the mirror.

I'm imagining this.

Aren't I?

The spider crashes in the sink bowl, leaving a streak of my blood in its wake, boogying its legs.

The left side of my face is a hole for the wind to blow straight into my brain.

Whispers . . . whispers I can't make sense of. Whispers and the taste of blood, and then bile, roaring up my throat. Me, bending over the sink to throw it up. A cockroach squiggling out the drain to greet me.

One roach, two roaches, three roaches. Four. Skittering up the basin with urgency.

"Oh . . . my God . . ."

It's like . . . a flood of roaches escaping some colony hidden in the pipes of my house.

Is this real?

"What's happening?" I scream to the sky, like God will answer me. Like he ever has.

I stagger back and fall on my butt and reach for the cabinet under the sink—backward and forward at once. My body doesn't know what to do.

Sawyer is watching himself in the mirror, staring at an empty reflection. "I believe you took something that belongs to me."

There must be some cleaner I can spray them with. The cockroaches spread. *Yes, there must be a tub cleaner that should do the trick and kill them . . .*

"Why would you do that, Jake? What are you hoping to find in the pages of that book? An explanation for why I thought to kill? Why I keep killing? Don't you think you could just ask me instead of going behind my back?"

"You never . . ." There are so many roaches. "You never talk to me normally." Roaches falling like BASE jumpers to the floor, spreading across it, on a mission, it seems, to fill the gaps in the tile—to eat the whole bathroom alive. "Get the fuck out of my house." My voice is low and clear.

Sawyer snaps to face me as a wind rushes through the space, blowing him backward, smearing his visibility through the cool air.

"Jake!"

A fist explodes against the door. I grab the doorknob and pull myself to my feet as a roach skitters up my naked leg.

Benji bangs the door while I shake all over. "Hey, Jake! You wanna *shut up*?"

"You want to know why I killed them?" Sawyer's struggling to stay in one piece, with his eyes sinking through the veins behind his face and gashes tearing into his arm, sending a smoke of blood into the air.

The banishing . . . it kind of worked that time.

It's kind of working.

"I killed them because they hated people like us. They hated *gay* people. People who hate gay people don't deserve to be here. Don't you think that?"

I know what he wants—to be in my head. But I'm in control now, and as I blink at the walls, at the roaches, their guts splatter and evaporate, like Sawyer's skin. I can make this stop happening. My eyelids are a pair of Whac-A-Mole mallets tied to their life spans.

I find myself in the mirror again—kinky curls, brown eyes and skin. Back to normal.

No roaches.

There were never any roaches.

I imagined them. Sawyer imagined them . . . for me?

There he is, still watching me from the other side of the bathroom, like he's waiting for an answer. And the roaches crawl up the side of his face, disappearing into his ears, hair, and head.

A grin flashes across his face, and his expression softens, like he's warmed to me now and wants to just be friends. "Don't you agree? Don't you think everyone who wants to keep you from Allister deserves to die?"

"GET OUT OF MY HOUSE!"

The shout sends ecto-mist ripping through his body so he rips apart at the cheeks and chest, his body splitting open at the neck and knees, until he pops in a burst of red smoke and then exits through the crevices of the door.

The shower curtain flaps like a sail, and the hinges rattle behind him.

I want to believe that's the end.

I escape the bathroom, enter my room, collapse on the bed, and tuck myself under the covers. The night darkens.

If he gets into my head again like that, I will lose. My ear is still sore from that wraith spider, and my skin crawling from those roaches.

The bugs . . . the bugs he played with in the forest, which he was so upset with his sister for throwing out. That memory forms a source of his strength and his terror now. He can raise it at will and use it against me.

I rise out of bed and swipe the book out from under it. If I get into his head, I could know what to expect. None of his tricks would surprise me, because I'd know everything he wrote about. And I'd always be one step ahead.

I don't have much longer, because I can't take much more of this.

I'm nearly at the end of the book—just a few entries left.

Nearly to the bottom of what turned him into the monster he is today.

SAWYER

Dear Diary,

I don't know what day it is. This may be the account of the end of my life. But I'm not sure yet. Today went very badly. I stayed home. Wore the XL shirt from Lanier Lake Vacation Bible School all day because it reminded me of the gown I wore in the clinic. Felt too depressed to move, but I went to the couch when Uncle Rod came to fix the ceiling fan.

He called me back into the room, so I mustered up the strength to return. He was on a little stepladder, fooling with the fan. Said he wanted me to watch him do it. Took the fan blades down. Didn't offer any instructions. Just wanted me to watch. Asked me about college. I told him I hadn't decided yet if I wanted to go. Spotted Momma's tote bag on the counter— she'd left it and would probably realize when she got to the diner.

Rod came off the ladder, said my momma was speaking up for me again and I couldn't let her keep doing that. I said I know, I gotta stand up for myself. He said if I leave this place he'll miss me, and I said me too, even though that was a lie—I don't care about my relationship with Rod at all.

He took off his tool belt and left the room. "Come on, Sawyer."

I followed, we stopped in the den, and he held out his arms for a hug. "Bring it in."

I know Uncle Rod isn't a hugger. I wasn't thinking. Just doing what he said. So we hugged.

I don't think Rod has friends.

He stuck his fingers through my belt loops and unbuttoned my pants. "Just relax."

I thought for some reason of when I went fishing with Bill. We caught fish and just watched them flop on the deck with the hook stabbing their lip, throwing them back when they were almost out of breath.

Rod's fingers grabbed my hip bone and guided me to the couch. Unzipped his own pants behind me.

"I have to go to the bathroom." I was gonna throw up and couldn't do it on Momma's couch.

"Don't worry, Sawyer," he said. "It'll be fine."

"Can we go to my room?"

He put his hand around my mouth. "Shh." His beer breath sprayed across my ear.

The hot taste of the roast beef I had earlier surged in my throat. "Please, can we move?"

Finally, he agreed to move.

I heard the bugs through the walls of the house. They should've been in their little holes. It was getting cold. But the cicadas were thriving, chirping like they were cheering someone on. And I wondered which of us—me or Rod—deserved to be punished as the whole forest hummed with the throttle of revenge.

Walking down that tunnel to my room with his hand on my shoulder was the last moment I was free. My jeans were still bunched around my ankles, so I had to waddle. I thought I would trip. Rod's hands would not let me go.

In the room, I broke for the closet with such speed he had to let go.

"Sawyer!" He yelled at me like I was his dog who'd escaped a leash.

I dove for the guns in my closet and grabbed what I could.

I swung it around and hit him in the jaw. He stumbled backward with his hand on his chin. I came out of the closet, AR-15 trained at his forehead.

"Back away from me," I commanded.

He did, holding up his hands, smiling nervously. "Sawyer . . . come on now . . ."

I told him to take off his clothes. The words came out in a panic. I didn't know the next thing to do.

"Sawyer . . ." He took off his shirt. His body was pale. His hair wrapped around his navel like a parasitic snake. Nothing I'd ever want to see.

I began to lower the gun, but the taste of vomit came back.

"Drop it, Sawyer."

Momma had appeared in the doorway, forgotten tote bag strung over her shoulder. She was holding a revolver, and it was pointed at my head.

There were so many questions that no one around me had answers for.

Like, why do I exist? What is the purpose of me?

No one ever gave me a good reason to get out of bed every day.

"Drop the gun, Sawyer," Momma demanded, her voice shaking. "Now."

"I don't know what happened, Joy," Rod said, putting on his best scared face. "He just . . . He just turned on me like this."

My heart sank to the bottom of my chest. My momma looked back at me like I was a violent stranger, someone she'd never even seen. Believing every word of his lie.

I dragged the barrel down to point at Rod's kneecaps.

How many legs would you need to survive?

Momma's finger played at her trigger. "Sawyer . . . ," she warned.

I fired into Rod's kneecap, and blood splattered from his knee, like it was eager to leave him. Shells from my weapon jumped over my shoulder.

A little laugh came out. *Die,* I thought as his face twisted and he tipped to one side, a circus freak with a broken stilt.

A scream. A BANG! And my shoulder burst open in bloody strips of fabric. An ache screamed through my tendons, veins, and fingers.

A wispy trail of smoke curled out of Momma's weapon. Her arms rattled like maracas. She shot me, and her mouth dropped open like she couldn't believe what she'd done.

But I could.

I stormed past Momma, out of the room, as she pressed herself into the wall.

"Sawyer!" she cried, pained and pleading.

"Shoot me!" I screamed. "SHOOT ME ALREADY!"

It's what she always wanted, to get rid of her crazy son, and that was her chance to end me.

But she didn't. She let me run away. So I swiped the keys to Rod's truck off the den table. One arm was bleeding, the whole sleeve soaking up the blood. In my free hand, I held the gun.

And this is my final account. It's over.

Rod, how far would you have gone? Momma, are you ready to

tell every parent in Heritage who loses someone how you failed as a mother and shot your own son because he was trying to stop your brother from raping him?

Police: I'm about to take my AR-15 into my school and kill as many people as possible. I'm bleeding, can't even feel one arm, and I will bleed out and die alone in Rod's smelly truck. Mother doesn't want to take me to the hospital, so nobody will take me to the hospital. I'm going to die, and I'm not going quietly. No political statement or whatever. I don't give a fuck, but after everything, I am not gonna die alone. That's a rip-off. Life is not fair. Everyone will know it. Goodbye.

JAKE

Jake?" Ms. Kingston calls, snapping me to awareness.

You're at school, I remind myself. "Here."

Not in Sawyer's world. Not living the last journal entry before his death. Even though it's been wedged like a wonky nail in my brain pattern ever since I started reading it a few days ago.

Everything is tipping back and forth like a slow, depressing earthquake.

I feel bad for him, and afraid of him. I don't know what to make of those two feelings warring inside me, and maybe I just shouldn't have read the fucking thing or stolen it in the first place. Has it done me any good? I mean, knowing the details of his life has shown me what aggravates him. That gives me ammunition in dead world, provides the opportunity to turn his fears against him in a way that might kill him. But I barely know how to conjure things, and especially not how he can—not whips, not spiders, and especially not a swarm of cockroaches. And even if I could, what power would those projections wield against him, anyway?

I haven't been sleeping, just swinging through my two locations. School, home, school home school home—can't I go somewhere else? The sun comes and goes. The desks and counters and chairs and beds change. I can't focus on a single thing that's said to me, because I'm thinking of what I'll do to Sawyer when he comes back. What he'll do to me.

Ms. Kingston is still talking. "What's with the hood? Take it down, please."

I don't have time to argue. "I'm cold, though."

Nobody should be allowed to tell me what I get to wear. This morning I stood at my closet and reached past my blazer and dress shirts to snatch my hoodie off the hanger—one I rarely wear in public, and especially not with the hood up, for fear I'll get in trouble.

But today, I wanted to be comfortable. Something about being hunted by Sawyer Doon makes this schoolteacher lady feel . . . small.

"Jake," she says. "It's not cold in here."

"It is to me. I'm African American, ma'am. My homeostasis is not built for cold weather. So I feel it even though you guys don't."

A round of laughter follows. A few "whats?" I don't mind the attention. All I'm doing is telling the truth—I get colder because I'm Black. It's not that hard to understand.

Ms. Kingston is red, embarrassed, and intrigued. She tilts her head at me like I'm a curious creature under a microscope—one she could squash with the heel of her boot. It's an evil, dehumanizing, calculating stare. One practiced to strike intimidation into hearts like mine.

I stare back. There are worse things out there than falling out of favor with a white woman who graduated from a college because her family had the money to send her there.

I turn to look at Fiona, to see how she's processing all this, and find a gleeful smile on her face—she's living for it. She, too, is down to risk being pushed out of a room she was never wanted in to begin with. And that's why I love her.

"Um, anyway." Ms. Kingston rolls her eyes and gives up. "Back to the topic at hand. We're talking about *The Crucible* today."

She fills the center of the room, looking down at her little stack of papers. I notice how her gray turtleneck shrouds every piece of her torso, neck to waist, so only her hands and face are exposed. The hands look older than the face.

She reads something. "Raise your hand if you think the events of the play fulfill the spell Abigail cast in the woods with Tituba earlier on in the play."

Half the hands go up, and half stay down. Fiona's stays down, so I keep mine down. I haven't read the play. It's never worth it to fake it.

"Anyone care to elaborate on their choice?" Ms. Kingston says, surveying the room with boredom and then landing on Chad, who's whispering to his friend about something not at all related to the book. "Mr. Roberts?"

Chad snaps to face her. "Oh, sorry, what was that, ma'am?" People laugh—they love his little performance. "Wait, did you ask about Tituba? I think it was all her fault."

More chuckles. Ms. Kingston rolls her eyes, but there's a smirk on her face too.

She regains her composure and asks, "And why is it Tituba's fault?"

"Because everybody knows Tituba bewitched Abigail and forced her to do everything. It was obviously slave revenge." More laughter.

Like trapped spiders eating my heart from the inside out.

"Soooo," Chad goes on, knowing how each word will tear me down, relishing in it. "Tituba is basically manipulating everyone to turn against each other so she can enact world domination."

Black people are always the punch line of a joke—it's maybe

why none of the books we read have Black people in them unless they're slaves.

Ms. Kingston glances in my direction and then stands up straight, shaking her bangs out of her face a little. "Anyway, no—I don't think that's what Arthur Miller *actually* intended."

I love how we all just move on.

"It's English, right?" Chad takes up space, too much of it, really—always sits with his legs so wide everybody around him just has to adjust. One elbow is resting on Kristen—the girl to his left, who he's been dating since he broke up with Laura a week ago. "We're supposed to be able to make our own interpretations, right, because that's what English is for?" Chad says. "My impression is it was Tituba's fault. Think about it. Who would have known if it was Tituba?"

I take out one of the drawing pencils in the side of my book bag. I bring them because in my distraction I like to doodle. I put the pencil through my tiny sharpener and touch the tip. It's sharp as a needle. The page in front of me darkens as I outline a sketch of a spider.

"Very funny, Chad," Ms. Kingston says. "But that's not what Miller was trying to—"

"I had a taxi driver tell me all about the witches in Africa once. They look like regular Black ladies, but they're bad spirits. And it runs in their bloodline. They pass all that spirit-seeing stuff down through generations. Like, even African Americans have it."

Chad chose to sit pretty close to me today. He's very lucky Fiona is separating us. This can't keep going on. All this sitting back and letting him get away with it. How good it must feel to be like Sawyer. To just give people what they deserve. All I want to do is snap Chad Roberts's neck.

I'm so dizzy, Ms. Kingston shrinks and grows like she's in a funhouse mirror. Her voice sounds like it's coming from somewhere else. She's not going to defend me. She never would.

"Does anyone else have anything to say?"

Still, Chad answers. "I think Jake should speak," he says. "Since we're talking about slaves."

I'm done.

I pick up my pencil, lunge over Fiona, and stab Chad through the hand, like sticking a spear into the soil, but it's a pyramid of graphite digging between his index and middle knuckles.

Dark blood oozes like lava from his skin. I drive the pencil deeper and drag it, like I'm carving a pumpkin, so now his perfect, privileged body can taste what it's like to have something sharp and angry stuck inside it.

"Oh my God." Fiona scoots back from her chair and claps her hand over her mouth.

For a second, the classroom inhales a perfect silence. And then everyone else lurches back from their tables too, as if they could be my next victims. Which they could be. Because they're guilty too, for laughing. Assholes. All of them can die.

I push back from my chair and stand up, feeling the whole room flinch in unison.

I clasp my hands together, pace, and speak over Chad's earth-shattering scream. "I think it was actually a really evil white girl who manipulated Tituba into a bad situation—"

"AHHHHHHHHH!" It tears his throat to pieces.

Now I'm laughing, and I'm the only one. "I think Tituba probably wouldn't expect other human beings to be so trash to her for no reason." I love to hear my own thoughts out loud.

"Maybe Tituba never wanted to be part of the play in the first place." I pick up the book and flip through the old pages so they cast a breeze on my chin.

Ms. Kingston breaks for her desk like her life depends on it. At first, I think she's running for the window to jump out, abandon the class to my terror, but then she reaches up the wall above her desk—the little silver button like an out-facing belly button that will page the front office.

⁕

Chad passes me while I wait outside the principal's office. He's on his way to the nurse, and he doesn't even look my way because now he knows better.

A minute later, I'm sitting across from Mr. Ross. His hands are folded on his desk, and mine are in my lap. His forehead is a mountain of creases because I guess he's perplexed by me.

"What am I supposed to do about this?" Mr. Ross asks, and his eyes flit down to the bloody pencil resting on a paper towel between us. "What do you propose?"

"I don't know. You're the principal—not me."

He leans forward. "Well, my first thought is to call the police, but then they'll say I'm racially profiling you. I'd really love to hear your suggestion for what you think is right."

The world has not stopped spinning. I don't know what Sawyer will do next, and there are bigger things at stake than this racist school and Mr. Ross's reputation. Fuck his reputation and fuck his school.

"I'm waiting," he says.

"I don't know what you should do. You have to decide for yourself what you should do."

Mr. Ross blinks in confusion or offense. "Excuse me?"

"Since it's your school, and you're basically in control of what happens to everyone in it, you get to decide."

"What are you implying?"

"I'm implying it doesn't matter what I say. Chad started it and I *defended* myself."

"Defended yourself? But you're not the one who had this"— Mr. Ross picks up the pencil and drops it—"buried in *your hand*." Mr. Ross recoils a bit from me, like he doesn't know what I'll do next. "What's gotten into you lately? You're behaving just like your brother."

I've barely said two words to this man before. Whenever I'm sent to his office, he discovers the teacher was the one tripping. There's no rhyme or reason to the way I'm treated here. So he gives me a fake talking-to and sends me on my way.

I had more than enough reason to put that pencil through Chad's hand. I'm sick of his shit. Now he'll mind his own and stop fucking looking at me all the time.

"Chad has been bullying me all year." My voice is a whisper— it doesn't capture a modicum of the desperate anger I feel. "And no one cares."

"I never heard about this."

"Because you wouldn't care."

I am tired of accepting that I have no power. When do I get a chance to retaliate against the things that make me feel angry or dehumanized? When do I get to say when's when?

Mr. Ross leans back and rubs his hand along his chin. "You've assaulted a student. So, you'll be questioned by the police and given disciplinary action. Chad's family could press charges."

"I understand."

"Now, I'm not a racist—"

"What does that have to do with anything?"

"—but you understand you chose violence before seeking help for your bullying problem."

"No one would have cared—what don't you hear about *no one would have cared*?"

"Okay, son, you need to calm down."

There's . . . alcohol on his breath. Smells just like that stuff Grady gave me. I'm sure Mr. Ross keeps bottles in his minifridge to make his faculty meetings easier. I can see him in front of a classroom of teachers, when we've all gone home, giving some milquetoast antiracism training.

"I got rid of a distraction." My voice is quiet, but there's pride in it because at last I've taken matters into my own hands.

"Got rid of?" Ross repeats, and the words make me cringe when he says them.

I could see why Ms. Kingston would be worried about the threat I posed to her class. She should be. There's a violent edge in me, a snap reflex I didn't even realize was there. I worked so hard, so long to keep it repressed. But this darkness I've pushed down is building to a climax because I've left it too long to build in silence. I understand why someone would do what Sawyer did, in a situation where it was the only choice.

No one can touch me. Not even the teachers. Not even the principal.

Mr. Ross looks at the minifridge behind him, like he's ready to pour a shot of whiskey, and then back to me, like he's decided against it. "I want to help both of you get past this. But there are rules. And you technically started it."

Mr. Ross would only lift a finger to help me if it were the most convenient thing to do, and truth is, here at this school, I'm just a little bit inconvenient. It's amazing how many people don't want to look racist and how few care about not actually being it.

"So, *I* will face consequences, and Chad will face nothing." It's the professional, concise recap of our meeting that he refuses to phrase in that way.

Ross looks bewildered still, like the panic of losing control of this interaction will drive him to insanity. "I . . . didn't say that. Don't put words in my mouth."

Be driven to insanity, you pathetic excuse for a principal. "But you implied it, Mr. Ross." Still respectful. Always respectful. "I'm not who this school is interested in protecting. So, at the end of the day, it doesn't matter what I do."

I get up so fast the chair falls over behind me, but I don't bother picking it up. It's a miracle I've stayed as calm as I have.

I storm out of the office, and as the door swings shut behind me, I hear Mr. Ross calling, "Jake. Jake! Sit down! We're not done here!"

He's wrong about that. We are very much done here. And I'm tired of sitting down.

SAWYER

I shot myself in the lobby of my school, in between the principal's and vice principal's office. I stopped existing. I must have.

I came back to the scene of my suicide, bullets exploding through my head as cops in helmets with rifles stormed the four doorways, sunlight framing their shadows.

I locked in the nightmare of dying via bullet wound over and over.

There was a voice that made me do it.

Now, it hissed. I shot myself. *Now,* it hissed when the blackness cleared again, in front of those doors where the light spilled in, highlighting shadows of police.

Now. The whispering voice pushed me in whatever direction it chose. It insisted that my death be on replay.

For a while I resigned from a fight that felt impossible to best. On the dark outskirts of my death moment, beyond that terrorized hallway, was a blackness I couldn't name. A darkness so deep I'd never find myself in it.

I chose to go toward it.

I remembered the people who should have been in front of my gun but weren't. And I freed myself and found myself surrounded by bodies of red mist, which shaped themselves into the images of my enemies. There were Rod and Bill, standing in the backyard. My sister throwing my bug factory into the river and laughing at my pain. The mist carried the pain of the world in little blinks of light and smoke. I saw Kieran Waters dying, the essence of his organs, bones, and skin picking themselves away in starlight.

I was born of their memory and my vengeance against them. I remembered who I was.

And the creatures showed themselves to me, wandering toward me from all directions of the darkness, like my rebirth called to them. Amphibious gray monsters whose legs bent like spiders'.

I followed them into the world, and it appeared to me as it did them, in the places of worst destruction. The highway dividers where cars careened off the road and people died. Hospital beds, where there were tears to lick off the faces of grieving mothers. Always pulling the thick air that trails off humans like gun smoke into my lungs, using it as food.

I learned from them. To find the most miserable, tortured creatures, the ones looking to escape from their realities, and I attach to their pain, their weeping, their doubtful silence.

And my fingers find light switches and turn them off, just to see the fear curl off their necks. Bikers pedal down busy streets and are launched before a moving car by way of my violent wind. From their injury and the chaos of pedestrians and police, I absorb the hot red panic, which fills the street like a smoke bomb.

It hits my head like a rush of oxygen, fills my lungs with vitality, makes my hands shake and turn opaquer, adds complexion to my skin. The pain, the rage, the suffering brings me back.

Jake, when he's hurt, burns like both the darkest and brightest point of light in the universe. A walking wash of indigo blue like a potion that transcends every universe.

I will have him for myself.

JAKE

I have eight missed calls from Mom. The school must be calling her. She must know what happened and that her son is violent, which means I can't go home.

So I walk in circles around my neighborhood, hands in my pockets. A ghoul tracks me down every avenue, passing through parked cars and fences, speeding up as I do, refusing to let me go.

I haven't eaten since breakfast. I should be hungry, but I'm sick.

How could I ever show my face in that school again?

I'm ashamed.

On the patch of wet grass between two roads, I turn around and face the monster.

"LEAVE ME ALONE!" My voice is a mad roar.

A storm starts in the echo of my scream. Rain dots the asphalt, the spots getting bigger and bigger, beating down the blades of grass and tickling my fingers.

The ghoul smiles wide. Drool leaks thick and viscous from its jaw. It knows what I've said, and it refuses. It just likes to taunt me and see me suffer.

As the storm starts, I pull down my hood, raise my face to

the sky, and greet the full force of the thrashing water. A vein of lightning rips above me, making a *CRACK* as it strikes something. A tree or a pole.

I wouldn't mind if it struck me next.

✛

At home, I swipe the diary from my room, take it outside under the awning of the roof, and burn it with the long lighter. It heals me to watch the leather and pages curl and blacken.

I go back into the house, dark except for the living room lamplight. Mom's waiting there on the couch, with her hands clasped between her legs.

I can tell she knows. I try to go for the stairs to avoid the whole conversation, but she stops me.

"Jake. Come here."

I meet her in the living room, looking at the carpet because I can't bear to look at her.

"The school called me today to tell me you were suspended ..."

I don't recognize what I did, but I feel like I was set up to do it.

" ... because you stabbed your classmate?" Mom is horrified and confused.

I have nothing to say. I can't believe who I am, but I also can't believe who other people are.

"I spent the better part of tonight begging the boy's parents not to press charges. What is going on with you?"

"I had to," I tell her. "It was the only way."

"The only way to what?"

"To defend myself."

"Against what? What's going on?"

"He was calling me a slave, and the teacher wasn't doing anything."

Mom raises her eyebrows. She doesn't say anything at first, and then: "Has this been going on for a while?"

"Yes, it's been going on forever."

"And you let this get to the point of physical violence. Why didn't you tell me?"

"I couldn't. I—I—I—" I'm a stuttering mess, and feeling hysterical, and the storm outside is cutting off my voice, so I can barely even hear myself. "I just wanted to handle it on my own."

"You what?" She tilts her ear to me. "You're mumbling, Jake—I can't hear you."

Nobody can. The balloon in my chest—it's being pumped with more helium than it can handle. I've never been able to talk to Mom about anything because she's never been there. Only halfway there. And it doesn't matter why I didn't do what I didn't do now that I look like a maniac who attacked somebody.

When I don't say anything, she keeps going. "You couldn't talk to anyone at the school about it before assaulting your classmate?"

As if I could talk to anyone at school. As if I wasn't already the villain there to begin with. "You just expect me to be perfect all the time. And nobody listens to me."

"What do you mean no one listens to you, Jake?"

"They don't . . ."

And the one time I stand up for myself, the blame falls on me, and everything that Chad has done to me all year, the way he's taunted me, doesn't matter.

The balloon in my chest is about to pop.

"You never cared when Dad was hitting me."

Mom goes still, like my words have frozen her. "Is that what this is about?"

I remember her watching him beat me after I brought the

magazine home. Watching as he choked me into the wall—she just stood there and watched, stone-faced, like there was nothing she could do. Like I deserved it.

"You didn't care." My voice is a whisper.

"Jake . . ."

"You didn't CARE!" I bolt out of the living room, tear open the front door, and run into the rain without closing it behind me.

If she's calling me, I can't hear her.

I just have to run. Down the avenues. Out of the subdivision and into the streets.

I don't know why when I'm sad, my first impulse is to run back to places that make me sadder. But that's what I do—I can't help but go back to where it happened.

··┊··

Fifteen minutes later I'm at the park joined to Woburn Drive, my old neighborhood in South Clark City. Here the potholes will blow out your tires, but the parks and recreation centers are nicely kept.

I guess I was raised here because those big grassy spaces are supposed to be good for kids. We all came out to this park to play—me and my best friend, Jalen Grey; Benji, Trevon, and Jeffrey. Benji stayed in touch with them after the divorce. I didn't. I guess it was a convenience thing. I hung out with them because there was no one else.

I always do that. Why do I always do that?

The park is behind a station of townhomes, where the backyards slope into a basketball court and a fenced-in playground. Inside the playground are a swing set, seesaw, and carousel.

I remember playing b-ball on the court next door. I was best at three-pointers. Jalen was better at layups. He would lift the bottom of his shirt to wipe sweat off his face whenever he made a basket. He always took off his shirt when it got too hot, revealing his strong back, the two squares of muscle where all I had were shoulder blades. And his spine, like a canal, caught his sweat.

I couldn't look away then and can't stop thinking about it now. It always comes back to me, how stupid I was for sticking that note in his pocket. *Do you like me?* it read.

At fourteen, when I realized I was gay, I picked up a magazine with a transgender woman on the cover on my way out of the gas station after school. It was Loretta Moore, the star of a comedy I'd gotten around to watching.

I'd seen Dad go through my things and burn what he didn't like. There was to be no witchcraft or wizardry. No ghouls, demons, or wendigos. Only Jesus Christ.

Darcy Carter, Arnold Chase, Koba Kaseem—all my favorite heroes went up in flames when he found out I'd been reading them.

He found the magazine just as fast.

"JAKE!" he bellowed, his volume shaking the house.

I found him in the living room, holding up the magazine. "WHAT IS THIS?"

The cover was ripped down the middle, across Loretta's face.

My voice didn't work. His voice left no room for it. I was shaking. He didn't need his fists to hurt me. The volume and the look sent sheer terror through my being. Still, his fists hit my face, neck, and stomach like blocks of hail. I left the house bloody faced, stomach upside down. He never said I'd have to go, but I couldn't stay. Now he knew for sure. I am gay.

I ran to the park. I swung on the swing, dragging my feet through the dirt, and I texted Grandma. She came to pick me up, gave me leftover dinner, let me rest on the couch.

Grandma's house is where I learned to fall on hard times. It's where I learned about art and cooking and culture. In her living room hangs a painting of six-year-old Ruby Bridges being escorted to school by four men in suits, the word NIGGER scrawled on the concrete wall behind her.

"That's how I want you to walk into that school every day," Grandma told me after I got into St. Clair, in the summer after ninth grade. "Head high," she said. "No matter what they say to you, you walk in there with pride and you get your education. Because nobody can take that away from you."

I open the fence and walk into the playground, my feet falling silently on the wood chips and mud. The fog in the thicket beyond the fence is parasitic. A shadow of trees hangs over me, like a jungle canopy, clawing at the darkness, hissing in the wind.

The carousel platform is a pie of fading blue, yellow, and red. The bars perch from a post in the center, like spiders' legs.

The wheel starts to spin when I sit on the flimsy wood.

"It's okay," I whisper.

No, it isn't. I want to curl up and die.

Sinking into my hood, I bring my knees to my chest. Lightning assaults my periphery and frames the silhouette of a ghoul watching me from the top of the hill. It's not scary to me now that I've seen the lifeless creatures enough places. I know the devil's workers want me dead, and it doesn't bother me.

A gust blows the carousel into motion, and I'm spinning. It's . . . dizzying.

Is that just one ghoul? Or is there one there by the picnic benches too? The swing set? The slide?

I can't tell if I'm facing just one ghoul or many.

I push my foot into the ground and spin myself faster and faster.

Can't go back to school, assaulted a kid over a slave joke. Can't go home, failed my mom.

Eyes shut, I hope for a pleasant dream. To drift off somewhere better.

"Is it too much to ask I not be haunted all the time?" I whisper to the particles of luminescent dust fizzing at my fingertips, as if they're my connection to God.

"Can't I have a crush at school, even if it's a boy? *Can't I just be a kid?*"

Or am I doomed to lurk in darkness? Prisoner to evil?

The questions go on, but each one gets quieter until they are barely heard, not even by me.

What did I do wrong?

What did I do?

⁘

I wake up in pitch-black darkness—darkness that makes me question if I'm awake and if I'm really here. I can't remember the moment I passed out on the carousel. Just endless existential questions blurring into white noise, which faded, at some point, into blackness.

I lift to a sitting position and place my hands on the ground beneath me, where they sink as if in sand. A black sand.

Ecto-mist forms a ring of cold fire on the ground around me, snapping in sparks of light blue. The ring expands, growing in density and range, covering everything. Shapes rise from it—glittering bodies forming themselves from foot to pelvis to head.

Glittering people in aprons and headscarves, tunics and turbans, boots and berets. Top hats and church hats and flapper dresses. People are running with knapsacks, thrashing the reins on horses, each shape there and then gone, making way for new ones.

They grow as they move, the mist making them denser, bigger. The mist starts to rumble with a hum of voices, like a church congregation at the end of the service.

The figures fade until there are twelve left. Each is the height of a doorway, with muskets, machine guns, daggers, and sabers in their hands. They surround me like a tornado getting tighter at the center, and I collapse to my knees, hands held up in front of me.

Please don't kill me.

But they stop in a close circle before touching me, casting me in a ring of light.

I pull my forearms from in front of my eyes. They're looking not at me but at one another. They turn to face the opposite direction, one by one, flipping like telepathic dominoes, connected to the movement of each other. Only one stays facing my direction—a man whose mist constellation forms the suggestions of a plaid shirt open over his ribbed tank top. Loose pants wave around the ankles, just above his sandals.

The man kneels in front of me so that his head is closer to my head, I guess to approach me on the same level. Honestly, it's just terrifying because he's the size of a monument. He could bite my head off if he wanted to.

"Jake . . ." His voice shakes me from the inside out.

The mist changes shape. It pulls off the giant figures like dandelion petals in a strong gust of wind. The mist forms around my body, breathes into me, puts gusto in my chest and strength in my bones.

How does he know my name? Where am I? Who are they?

The mist man shrinks down, closer to my size. "Jake?" he says. "What are you doing here?"

His face, even constructed in stars, obstructed in dust, looks familiar to me. I've seen him in picture frames and photo albums, mostly around Grandma's house. Real smooth OG, always seen in beach shorts with a book and a pencil, or in a classy getup—suspenders, shiny shoes, and cigars. He's always with Mom or Auntie Sheryl in the pictures. It's their dad, who died when I was too young to remember.

And now, here he is. "Grandpa?" I say.

"You got something evil chasing you," he warns me, shaking his head slightly, like there's no time for introductions. "An evil that's about to rip that good spirit in two."

"What are you talking about?"

"I'm talkin' 'bout you, sleepin' on a playground, all ready to let *Satan* win."

A gray fog curls off the ground outside the circle, and new shapes form in the matter of black clouds, like the dust from a bomb explosion. Stringy limbs, emaciated midsections, bald, eyeless heads—the ghouls. They walk around the circle, around my circle, like they're searching for a way to sneak in and get me. One of the protectors—one with a saber—lashes out and slices the arm of a ghoul. Black fluid leaks out of its sallow skin as it crouches backward, hissing through the darkness.

This dust of glittering blue and the fireflies synchronized in airborne ballets around me . . . they were never mindless souls. They were conscious people all along.

This must be it. The world Ms. Josette told me about, which only reveals itself when it wants to. So . . . if they were here all along, why didn't they visit me sooner? I could've used a little help from the gods before now. Or a lot.

"You don't want to go out like that—trust me." Grandpa's voice is so human it's almost familiar, and so strong my skin vibrates when he talks. "You want a peaceful passing, so peaceful the demons don't even notice when you 'bout to be gone."

Part of me always thought being a good person would protect me from eternal torment. Call it being raised in the church, where Dad dragged us every Sunday growing up.

The reason I never retaliated against Chad, or clapped back at my teachers, or confronted Benji or Mom . . . it's because I felt like every single thing I did had to be perfect, or else I'd suffer forever once I died.

River must exist as one of these figures now. Someone with better abilities she gained after fighting Sawyer. I hope she got in touch with her mom.

"So . . . if I die here and now, I become like you?"

"You don't want that . . ."

"But what if I do?" I tour the circle of bodies, inspecting the backs of the warriors in my tribe—their Afros, leather jackets, and bullet belts. Silk linen cape jackets, muskets and sabers and cowboy boots. "No offense, Grandpa, but this seems like a much cooler place to be. Being able to just kick it with my ancestors? Why wouldn't I want this?"

"Because we don't just *kick it*, boy," he announces in a tone that lets me know, in one swift sentence, that I need to shut up. "You must make a choice, and it is an important one. I can't tell you how to run your life—you're a man now. But I would encourage you to continue it so that you have better tools to assist our family moving forward."

I won't be able to continue our family, though. Because I don't like girls. And it's always been that thing telling me I won't make it anywhere after I die, except hell.

Dad wanted me to talk like him and do everything just like him.

The Sunday after the magazine incident, when the pastor at his church asked the congregation if anyone needed special prayers, Dad carried me to the pulpit and told the pastor something evil was in my body. I remember his sweaty hand on my forehead, his quavering voice—"Watch over this boy, Lord, your child, Lord, release the evil from his bones, Lord." The congregation muttered, "Yes, Lord," "Hallelujah, Jesus," to pray the gay away.

Falling for another boy didn't come into the question, because it was out of the question.

And yet, Allister makes me happier than anyone ever has. He texted me the other day to ask if I was good, since I'd avoided him at lunch. And I never responded. I want him to get his answer.

"Will I make it here if I'm gay?" I ask—it comes out before I can stop it.

Everything I say has felt less reviewed lately, less rehearsed. I'm getting comfortable saying what I feel. And now, that relaxed thought-word relationship is about to fuck my whole life up, because I just told a godly ancestral being that I'm a homosexual.

Probably should have thought that one through first. It's the first time I've acknowledged it out loud, and it feels like a dirty word.

I see my father's fist closing in on my face, again and again—an aggressive, unstoppable demolition ball. The mist around my arms shapes into the conjuring of a new man in front of me—a familiar wraith of blue and black.

Don't you ever bring something like this up in my house again! he screams. *FAGGOT!*

My head smacks the mantel of my memory as he hits me in the eye. I feel it burst all over again, the way it did then, and my windpipe crushes in his grip, against the wall in our living room.

I drop to my knees, wrapping my hands around the angry wrist.

Help me, I pray to no one in particular, the same way I did in those moments he beat me.

That time, I got no answer. This time, a voice responds.

"Let go of it," it says.

A hot wind peels my father's hands away.

I hold my hands out, palms facing the ground. My fingernails swim in a starry glitter. It's like the fist buried itself in my nails. The spirits absorbed into a manicure.

A river of purple light tears across the blackness up above. Streamers of pink gas stretch like ribbons across the sky. Purple spinners, waterfalls of vibrant green, stars exploding in shades of light blue and white. A whole new galaxy of color.

Grandpa is smiling. Light shines like diamond carats from his mouth. And then he starts laughing. Laughing and laughing, bending his neck back laughing, slapping his knee.

I realize he's not laughing with me, because I'm not laughing. He's laughing *at me*.

"If you think that changes sum'n about all this, then you STU-PID, boy! It's been Black folks like you, Jake, since it's been Black folks—you know you sound like a fool. Because when you gone, it's gon' be a whole lot more just like you to be born. And they will know who you were and know that it's okay to live, because *you* lived before them."

I'm so relieved. Grandpa treats me well. How did he treat my gay ancestors? When it wasn't okay with anybody? Could I find my people here, in this universe? There'd be so much to ask. So many stories to lead me, to teach me it's okay. That there's joy to be found and a life to be discovered and rediscovered.

I'm afraid of the person I'm becoming. I put a pencil through a guy's hand and laughed. My emotions? Too big, too all-at-once for me to manage. Who knows what I'll do next? What if I fall off the deep end? Open fire on my class? I don't trust myself anymore. And if I lose myself . . . I'll never be visited by my ancestors again. This is a place for heroes. And they'd never welcome me in.

The carousel manifests outside of the ancestral circle and I find myself lying with my legs bent at the knees. My head is crooked against the wheel, like it's two inches from snapping, and my arm is outstretched like I'm already dead. A ghoul is spinning the carousel with one finger, keeping it at the pace of a cranked wooden music box, like it's turning the dial on my life span.

How long do I have to live?

It creates such a spectacle—dying out in the open. Imagine I died here. A soccer mom or a man with a leaf blower or a kid walking his dog would discover my hard body on the carousel, dead in a playground, and their innocence would be ruined forever. The park would be ruined. No more laughter and fun. Just a wake of devastation.

Mom would hear the news and shatter like a busted light. Giving up here would be so unfair to her. She'd have to deal with it after. So I can't do it. She doesn't always hear me, but she loves me.

I push my shoulders back and my chest out. It only seems respectful to match the stance of my grandfather when I speak to him. To mirror his power and strength as best I can.

"I'm gonna fight him," I announce.

My ancestors snap to formation with a collective hoot, all crossing one fist over their chest at once, taking hold of the quivers, bullet belts, or their own hearts, the breath in their chests. They're with me. If nothing else, I can go back to the Here and live in peace knowing something glorious awaits me on this side of fate. That alone gives me purpose. That alone gives me fight.

The air oscillates, ripples, and darkens around everything, like the universe has plunged underwater. Grandpa's shiny shoes twinkle into nothing, followed by his legs, his waist. My ancestors wither with him, one by one, and then they're gone, the mist bringing them back to their amorphous shapes. The light disperses toward me, framing my hands in the blue light of my soul aura. The aura of all of their souls.

"Don't let me catch you thinkin' 'bout givin' up again . . ." My grandfather's voice fades like a train engine down a railroad.

"I won't," I tell him. It's more a hope than a promise. I can't make any promises.

My ancestors abandon me to a blackness. A coven of ghouls closes in to fill their places, arms out, fingers curling like falcon talons.

I cross my arms over my head as their shadows descend, and their roars blow apart the darkness.

⁘

My eyes spring open as a wave of cold, wet air shoots through my throat.

I'm on the carousel again, with my legs curled up and my arms tucked under my head. The carousel is perfectly still, and there's someone sitting cross-legged next to me.

"Sucks to know your family's not really there for you."

I recognize his voice immediately. Powerful and tinged with uncertainty.

Here I am again. The swing set. The fence. The court and trees beyond it.

I'm in no hurry to jump off the carousel. Sawyer thrives on my fear. I refuse to let him see it.

"You watch me everywhere I go." Finally, my voice comes out in full depth.

He turns to face me. "Bold of you to assume that."

"You follow me everywhere."

"You're a medium. Any sensible ghost would."

A frigid wind blows through the park, stirring the maple leaves and pine needles into sinister whispers.

"What are you waiting for?" His voice comes like a pitchfork, prodding and sharp. "Banish me, medium." As he stands, pieces of mist spiral around his arms and legs. "Make me go away. Make the whole country forget me. Make them stop showing my face on the news or shivering when they speak my name. Make them stop trembling under the shadow of my memory. Write me out of existence . . . if you have that power."

"What happened to Kieran Waters?" I ask.

A face with a desperate mouth pulls from Sawyer's skin, turning him, momentarily, into a two-headed creature. Sawyer shakes his head and sucks the soul back into his cheeks.

He's mastered the art of trapping traveling bodies between this world and the next.

The carousel starts to spin, slowly at first, and then fast. The park moves behind him—behind both of us—and the fence becomes a blur of silver, a giant field of electric foil. I find my feet and grab on to the rail.

Eight dead . . . eight potential souls trapped inside one angry ghost.

"You absorbed the souls of your victims, and now they're fighting for a way out."

He half laughs. "Good luck to them—they have nowhere else to go." His voice is different now; it's lost its Southern intonation and turned into the dude-bro voice of a trust-fund white boy.

"How do you do it?"

"I suck up their life as it leaves their body. It's easy, Jake."

He leaps off the carousel and ends in a midair float. The fog and mist have grown so thick and wrapped so much around us that all we are is top halves.

Sawyer crosses to the swing set, and I follow. He presses down on the wooden seat and sits, not passing through it. "Funny thing is, I didn't want to do it." Strings of red energy wrap around his throat like a choker. "I didn't want to hurt anybody for real. Never planned to."

"Then why are you still doing this?"

"What else would I do? I'm trapped here—might as well make the most of it."

"Killing people is the most you can make of dead world?"

He's silent. His cold blue gaze shows no feeling, not even the emotions of the people he stole. If he gained control of my body, I'd become a murderer by the power of his wicked hand. My record would catch up to me, and he'd step out of me after running me straight into prison, because Sawyer can exist in either world but wants to live in mine.

I've been such a good target. If his mission is to induce fear to gain strength, it makes sense he would choose me.

But I know now I have power in dead world. The power of my ancestors.

And the wraiths—the choking hands from Sawyer's throat, and the whips—they only work on me because of my association with them. Because of my traumatic memory and the memory in my body. Not because they're dangerous.

If I can get inside his mind and know the things that trouble him, I can fight him with his own fears. I can conjure a wraith powerful enough to wipe him from existence.

"Have you ever thought that you don't have to do this?" I ask. "That maybe if you asked, I would help?"

He chuckles. "Sure, because you're dying to surrender your body to a murderer."

"Why do you have to murder? Something happens in the brain when you connect it with another one. You wouldn't just be you in my body, we'd be both of us."

"So you're offering me rehab."

"You obviously still need it. If this is all a social experiment to see how long it takes a nice guy to snap, why not just give me the snap reflex? Give me the sadistic mind that makes people not want to fuck with you—maybe *I could use it.* The final answer can't just be leaving people tormented or dead. What do you win?"

That glint of humanity erupts in him—the abandoned child that wants the same friendship as everybody else. It's exactly how I need him to be to defeat him. I have to get inside his head and access his most vulnerable thoughts. Master his motivations, his weaknesses, and his fears.

"Are you saying you wouldn't fight me if I possessed you right now?"

If it means stopping this cruel game before Allister gets hurt . . .

"I wouldn't fight you," I answer.

He doesn't need to hear it twice. Sawyer rushes into my skin and doesn't come out the other side.

SAWYER

His blood fills my arms like a Jacuzzi blaster.

And the park is vibrant now, free from that blackness on the outskirts of everything. Monkey bars, picnic tables, and thorny shrubs explode with color under the ice-white slice of moon.

I drop like a deadweight off the swing and into the wood chips. Each crawl to the carousel is like dragging a billion pounds. I become steady on my way up the railing. The wind is cold and nibbling and sways me from one side to another, up the concrete stairs, and back to the neighborhood.

The beauty of manual action. To move from place to place, knowing that where you came from and where you're going won't disappear. Everything is here. It's not going anywhere.

Back on the sidewalk, homes and roads spread out as far as I can see. I throw a wink and a smile at a SPEED LIMIT 15 sign. The age I was when Bill left.

I used to want a house like a normal kid, with a garage and neighbors. I wanted a mother who made dinner and sat with me to eat it. Yes, early on, I wanted that, to experience what it felt like.

⁛

When I arrive at Jake's home, I'm crying happy tears.

No one is on the main floor to see me rip the butcher's knife out the kitchen drawer.

I run upstairs. I barge into the brother's bedroom without knocking. I reach under his bed and steal his pistol. I'm halfway out the door when he realizes what I've taken.

"Jake? What the fuck are you doing?"

"I am not Jake."

I'm trotting down the stairs so fast I almost trip. He'll never catch me.

I'm jumping into the mother's truck. I'm sticking the key in the ignition, pulling off.

The brother yanks the door open behind me and tears into the driveway. "Hey! What the fuck?!"

I lose him in the rearview mirror and scream into the windshield, "SUCKER!"

The sweet rush of escape! The freedom.

The texture of the steering wheel, the smell of the leather.

The blackness of night extends beyond me. This world. I miss it. The time when simple things, like cars and seats, felt whole in and of themselves. No more fragments of a semiconscious world. No more relying on the mood swings of humans for energy. Just my own emotions, rip-roaring from my chest and through my body.

Destination: Heritage Hardware. An interstate dash from Clark City.

I enter the store, and thanks to Jake's nose, I feel drunk on the aromas of wood, oil, and paint. I drop a pair of garden gloves, matches, a jug of kerosene into a basket. At the cash register, I giggle like a kid in a toy store. The cashier is a nerd with a long neck and a receding hairline. Gives me a look as he rings up the items.

"Is there a problem?" I challenge him. My new voice is deeper. It's how I always felt I should've sounded.

He smiles and shakes his head. "No, sir."

That's what I thought.

I leave the store with a nod to the security guard and get back in my new truck. Never learned to drive, but it doesn't matter. If Jake dies, I will simply find another one to watch from the trees and strike down when I'm ready.

JAKE

My hands, twitching. My thoughts—loud, fast, angry, all at once. Images and places I've never seen before tear through my head. Two white men in a forest, one in a hunting cap, the other in a khaki sun hat.

I hate them. I'm coming for them.

How far are you willing to take this? A question like a pistol pops through the static in my head.

you're gonna pay you're gonna pay you're gonna pay you're gonna pay

His thoughts are like explosions on loop, and the turns turn themselves. The stop signs, wrong ways, speed limits—all of it just zips by, barely there. The speed bumps, traffic barriers, and all of it come second to the speed of this car.

SAWYER

The stoplights occur to me only after I've zipped through them. They had better be the right color because I am not stopping. If somebody gets hit, so be it.

STOP, screams a voice in my head—a prisoner held captive. *LET ME GO.*

don't tell me to relax don't tell me to relax don't tell me to relax

I never learned to read the signs anyway. Only ever operated an off-road vehicle one time with Bill, so if I die in this body, it won't even matter, because I have conquered death and know nothing is permanent, so there's nothing to be afraid of.

One of these lights in the darkness is the moon, in some stage of being there and then gone.

My heartbeat pumps me full of gasoline. The rhythm beats the walls of my chest like a ticking time bomb about to explode.

⁂

The damp walls of the outhouse, my sanctuary off the beaten path from my childhood home, are what I remember best. The ivy overgrowing so it crept inside. Moonlight snuck through a crescent at the top of the door when it was full. It twinkled on the glass jars, which tussled with tortured insects in the toilet hole—moths with no wings, daddies with no long legs. I pinched off their body parts with tweezers and suffocated them with their fallen brethren.

All I see is wood now. In this blackness, the walnuts, pines, maples, and oaks appear all by themselves. I see them struck by lightning, crushing houses and the people in them. Cars crashing into trees. Balconies collapsing in flame; people burning with them. Splinters poking out of children's fingers and shins—bleeding body parts detached from their people. Brown and red leaves floating everywhere.

I come from a family of tree lovers. Uncle Rod's cabin is up the bend of some unlabeled, unassuming forest in northern Georgia. I haven't seen him visit Annie and Momma, who still live in that house together. Annie's done nothing but sleep and cry since graduation. Momma just works, smokes cigarettes, and stares dead-eyed out of windows.

Every time I visit, she turns to the darkness to face me.

"Sawyer?" she gasps, and the sudden spark of light tears like a lightning bolt through my skin, blinding me.

Electrical ballasts, fluorescent bulbs, power boxes—they're my sworn mortal enemies. The aura of fear is weakest when people can see what's around them. I guess Momma doesn't know that, because she thinks that when I died, I died forever. Now whenever she tries to see me better, all she does is cast me out.

Rod let the family fall apart in the wake of his crimes. He left my aunt and my cousins.

He lives alone in this cabin, which I park in front of, on the road past the driveway. I drop the matchbox in my pocket and stick the kerosene bottle and gun into the back of my jeans so they're hidden under my sweater. After putting on the gloves, I walk up the driveway and down a walkway framed by bushes.

Then I'm on the front porch, practicing my breathing in the way Dr. Scott taught me.

The crickets thrum in the surrounding forest—the audience for my final act.

I knock at the door, and a loose bulb instantly flickers on above me. It's like he was watching for a stranger, anticipating one.

Haunting him as a poltergeist could never be enough. I've spent the past year dreaming of the moment I'd get to kill Rod, with real human hands, to christen a new body in his blood.

What would I say? What would make his final breaths hurt the worst? Now that I'm here, I can't remember any of that. Now that I'm in it, there isn't much to say—only things to do.

Rod answers the door with a defensive wince—shock and disgust because there's a Black boy on his property.

"Yes?" Rod says, already impatient. "Can I help you?"

He looks ready to pull a gun out from somewhere, but I got one in my waistband too, so I dare him.

I give him a once-over. Receding hairline, normal brown eyes, nose bent four different directions, stringy blond hair falling around his ears like corn silk. A beer belly through the tank, cheap cargo shorts, crusty feet, a stitched-up knee.

The sight of the kneecap I blew up brings an air of relaxation, of peace.

My moment of power.

My legacy.

"Hi, sir, my car broke down," I say, my voice measured. "My phone's dead, and I need some help making a call. If you could h—"

"No," he interrupts. "You know what time it is, man? It's almost twelve in the morning."

"My car broke down, sir."

"No."

Rod tries to slam the door, but I stop it with my hand. We shake there for a moment, him pushing the door harder and me holding it open.

This may be my only chance. I can't waste it.

I force the door open and stick the knife in his stomach.

"Excuse me, sir." I invite myself in. "If you'd just let me finish."

Rod stumbles backward, gasping and gaping at the knife handle jutting out of his stomach. I step over the threshold and close the door behind me, tenderly locking both locks.

Rod didn't mind it when he stole my last bit of innocence.

When he convinced my own mother to shoot me.

When he convinced me to shoot others and then myself.

There is something wrong with Uncle Rod. There must be something wrong with me too, since we share blood. I must be horrible by other people's standards, but strangely, I don't care, because it's how it must be, as a ghost, when all your strength comes from human weakness.

But even in life, you must kill people *before* they kill you, not after.

I press two fingers into his chest. He collapses on his back, legs and arms squirming like a centipede. He shuffles down the floor, toward the kitchen counter.

I step on the knife and drive it in, conjuring a clenching of teeth, a gasp of agony, a surge of blood.

"Just relax," I whisper. "Relax."

Rod turns on one side and drags himself toward the kitchen,

where the phone is. I lift one leg up and bring my foot down on the side of his face, so his head goes *SNAP!* against the floor.

He doesn't even manage a scream—only a stunned gasp. He turns on his back, and though he is breathing, his face is a disfiguration of red slop.

"No phones," I command, wrapping my hands under his armpits and pulling his body farther inside the living room. "No cops."

I'll be damned if you crawl to safety when I didn't have that choice.

I wander his place as he bleeds, keeping one eye on him the whole time.

A cabinet of guns. A hyena rug. A Confederate flag hung over the blinds so that everyone will know what he stands for. The man is unchanged.

✦

My third lesson came from Uncle Rod. He came to my room the night of my seventeenth birthday celebration and showed me how to build an AR-15.

"I want you to see that all this," he said, "is different parts. All this makes a weapon what it is."

It was the trigger guard, the pistol grip, the trunnion, the buttstock.

They looked so intricate hanging in his dining room cabinet. It was a dark and protective décor. I've always admired them in a way.

✦

I open the doors of the gun cabinet, brush my hand along the barrel of a black one with two grips and several holes in its design. The Sig Sauer MCX, whose nickname I can't remember but must be something like *Joy*. There is such beauty in the weapon, in its power and submission. How removed it is from the man that carries it, and yet acting in such violence nonetheless.

I take it off its hinges. Pop out the magazine. Load it with bullets. Just how Rod taught me when he thought his own lessons couldn't be used against him. Now he's on the kitchen floor, hands wrapped around a knife handle.

"Wh-wh-why?" Bloody spittle spatters from his mouth. "Why are you doing this?"

Gun on coffee table. Knee on floor, right by his side. I tilt my head so that our eyes connect.

"Because you're a rapist," I remind him.

Maybe he's forgotten, because his eyes widen like he's shocked. "Who are you?"

"God." I yank the knife out of his stomach and replace it in his thigh. Another gurgled scream—music to my ears. "Good to see your knee healed up."

"P-please stop," he begs.

I drive it into his ribs. "Relax, Rod. You don't have to do anything."

This time when he screams, I notice he's missing a tooth in the front. Did that fall out when I stepped on him? Or does Rod just have poor dental hygiene? I push back his lips and look inside because I genuinely want to know. He wrenches his head away from my hand.

"I said *RELAX*." I yank his face back toward me by the lips.

"Please . . ." A reddish clear tear spills from one eye. "I'll give you money—I won't tell."

By the blood pooling under him, it seems he's on the verge of death.

I grab the machine gun off the coffee table and point the barrel at his chest.

"Okay, game time," I say. "If you can guess my name, I won't shoot you."

"I don't know," Rod chokes. "*I don't know who you are!* Please don't do this."

"I said *guess.*"

"Uh, Jamal!" he screams. "Tyrone! Anthony, Malik, *fucking I don't know!*"

"Sawyer, actually."

Rod goes still and silent, as if he isn't bleeding. As if he's not been stabbed at all. When he speaks, his voice is clear.

"What did you say?"

"Sawyer Doon." I place one foot on his bloody stomach and watch his face contort. "Your favorite nephew."

"Sawyer?"

A fit of bullets explodes his body. A funny dance rattles his arms and legs.

He's dead in a second.

Giggling, I throw the gun across the floor. I skip around the house, tear his Confederate flag into strips, pull the gun cabinet off the wall, and tip it over. *BANG!* The glass goes everywhere.

I throw his candle holders through the windows. I smash his TV screen with the Sig Sauer.

Then the kerosene. I drench him in it. And the floors, tables, and countertops.

Once everything is slippery slick, I slide through each room and light the fluid, raising little bursts of flame in my wake.

The den, the dining room, the kitchen, the bathroom, the—

The . . . the burning fabric and the smell of flesh is unbearable . . . like knives digging up through my nostrils and sinking into my brain.

Fire engulfs the rooms, growing and growing, forming deadly clouds.

I cough, and blood lands at the inside and outside of my lips. In the middle of my glove.

My nose is leaking blood and my skin opening in little tears across my arms. The flame is eating me from the inside out without even touching me.

JAKE

We stumble across the floor, toward the door we came in through. Rod becomes crispy behind us, like a big burnt bit on a skillet fire. The flames have us dizzy and disoriented. My body feels like it's been set on fire, even though the fire hasn't touched it.

What the fuck is this?

Heat waves swim across our vision. Our eyes and heart burn like they've been set upon hot coals that are eating us from the inside out.

I think, *This is just what I need—for Sawyer to be panicked. I should fight back now, while he can't manage. But somewhere less obvious . . .*

Fuck, fuck, fuck, he thinks, so loudly he doesn't even hear my thoughts in our head.

He throws the door open and pulls us free from the house. A window explodes behind us, its glass shattering in bits along the porch as we stumble down the steps, across the lawn, gasping in the clean air.

Two ghouls pass us, going the opposite direction, likely drawn to the smell of Rod's rotting flesh. They phase through the walls of Rod's house as its wood is eaten alive.

SAWYER

When sawyer was twelve he played in his room with a doll named maxxy
she sat in a chair in the corner of gramma's house
sawyer asked if he could take it home and gramma said
    yes without a question
just wanted to make her grandson smile
he braided maxxy's black hair
and sat her in the closet and made her look beautiful
then one day she disappeared
come outside, bill said, i want you to see something
and there maxxy was again but not maxxy anymore—
    just a dead thing
burning in the fire pit out back
her hair roasting so the forest smelled of melting plastic
    and boy's tears
sawyer cried and bill and rod laughed together, toasting
    their beer in joy
loving every minute of it
these are for girls, bill said
no more hanging out at gramma's, rod said
and both laughed and mocked sawyer

now sawyer plays with guns and sets dolls on fire
now sawyer can't stand to feel on fire

⁜

Momma was the first one to teach me how to hold it on a lazy late afternoon in the third grade, when I was lying on my bed, watching a spider crawl up the sunbaked wall, thinking about nothing.

She knocked and came in. "Hey, Sawyer? Come here real fast. I wanna show you something."

We went out back, and Momma loaded up a cylinder.

"I'm telling Annie the same thing. If I'm not here and you see somebody strange out here you don't know, trying to get inside? You have my permission to shoot them. It's your Second Amendment right. It's self-defense."

The wind tickled the strands of blond hair around her ear as she squinted and then shot at a tree. I watched the bark explode as smoke trailed up from the barrel. Then she made me do it.

She put Bill up to teaching me to shoot a second time, age twelve. We shot at targets at an indoor shooting place. I flinched every time a bang exploded from my hands. The side of my face started simmering. A hot shell had bounced out the back of the gun and wedged between my glasses and face. I jumped out of the booth.

Bill came screaming at me. I'd dropped the gun.

"You don't treat a gun like that." He grabbed my arm like he was trying to break it loose. "You know better!"

The people near us turned around to glare at me.

I had the scar where my skin singed off for three years, and it took me just as long to return to the weapon and point it the right way.

I'm afraid this whole house will blow up, that the wood will crash under the pressure of the flame.

He is dead. I did it.

I pull out of the driveway and take off down the mountain, singing sweet freedom down the black lanes until my hands pull the steering wheel and twist, crashing the truck into a tree.

JAKE

A chaos of trees. Trees on fire, ghosts flattening under trees, cars rolling down hills and crashing into them. My soul body soars through the forest over all of this chaos, tumbling through scenes of destruction.

We tumble until we crash into a thick mound of dirt, glittering with ecto-mist. It stops us, and then I sink through it, my calves and hands disappearing under the forest floor. All around me, stems, roots, and woody vines curl up from the soil, sprouting flowers of red, white, and pink.

They die as quickly as they grow. My astral body is up to its armpits in dirt and branches. My physical body is up the hill, in the seat of the crashed truck, its limp head resting on the wheel, the airbag deflating under its chin.

Impact must've knocked Sawyer out too . . .

There he is. His soul took a different course, and now he's stumbling up the hill, the dark quicksand of dead world pulling at his shoes. Flares of smoke shape his flailing arms. Shadows of faces reach out from his forehead. Figments of arms reach out of his skin.

How many people . . . I think as I race to my feet. *How many people have you hurt?*

He thrashes like lightning up the hill, toward the truck. I push through the foliage, and it disappears around me in fizzles of green and red.

I push off from my feet, fly across the forest, and crash into him, our souls colliding like two physical properties as we nick the dying bark and spin to the ground. Splinters of light. My hands, aglow in pink and blue, clutching his hoodie like he'll sink through my fingers. We become swimmers in the ground of the forest, fighting to stay above the escaping earth. It's crawling with beetles and springtails, centipedes and worms—corpses and husks, skittering and cracking and decaying.

Sawyer claws at my face and drags his nails down it so the maggots and insects can burrow there.

We drown further into the earth, Sawyer with his hand on top of my head, twisting my neck into the dirt to push himself up. A chaos of bugs. Tiny legs burrowing into my ear cavities. My eyes disappearing into the earth, my throat choking up. They treat my eyes and nostrils as a home for their endless squiggling, their birthing and dying.

Inside the earth, my hand glows as a silver-blue hilt appears between my fingers and thumb. A blade springs from the hilt in an explosion of mist.

I sprout like a tree from the dirt and wave the sword over my head, cutting away dirt and brambles and striking Sawyer in one fell swoop.

With a hiss, he throws himself off me in a backward dive to his feet.

I stab the ancestral sword into the ground and push down on the hilt to force my way up. I sprout like a tree as a cloud of ecto-mist forms beneath my feet, giving me a solid place to stand on the shifting dirt. I pull the sword out, twirl it around my wrist, and dive for Sawyer.

I cut his face open, once across, opposite the direction his hair sweeps. His skin cracks. Pieces cake away like volcanic dirt. From under the skin, creepy-crawlies pop like bullet shells, squirming and simmering, fading into nothing.

He is made of the earth and bugs and trees. The forest and its creatures.

Chunks of skin return to Sawyer's lips, nose, and eyes, and I strike again, this time at the chest.

My weapon vanishes through a cloud of red smoke—he's gone. He's reborn again as a hand at my back. It pushes me beneath a falling tree that's tilting over slowly, in its death loop.

Chains of red and black rise up, catch me by my wrists and ankles, and pin me to the ground. The ancestral sword disappears in a blur of smoke. And the tree falls, its shadow coming over me. The ecto-mist sweeps across the forest in a glittering semicircle of ice blue, capturing the restraints at my wrists and exploding them, freeing me in flight.

I flip backward to safety just as the tree hits the ground in a burst of light.

I land on my feet with a new sword in hand and catch Sawyer racing up the hill.

My physical body is knocked out in the truck. I command myself to rejoin it, and a carpet of mist forms beneath me. It flies me up the hill, over Sawyer's head. I throw the sword toward him. It shanks one leg. His calf bursts into beads of red light. They escape like precious rubies down the sand and pull him lopsided into the earth.

I win.

He's dying behind me. The souls and earth eating him. The ecto-mist is teaming up with ghost ticks and leeches to feast on his flesh and make him obsolete.

My soul hits my body like a train car collision. I pull my face off the steering wheel, inhaling a cyclone of cold air.

Back to the road . . . back to civilization . . . back to people . . . to trees.

I snatch my hand out of my lap and yank the gearshift back. The wheels rev up, only to roll circles in the dirt.

"Come on, come on," I'm begging the truck, pushing the pedal to the floor so the vehicle operates at its most extreme power.

It veers into a clumsy backward swerve. I become a jangling dummy between the window and console. The truck wheels screech on the road, and it spins in a noisy circle.

I slam the brakes and stop, fingers wrapped around the wheel. Ahead is a patch of road, black with bright yellow lines. A place you'd catch a deer in the headlights half a second before it demolished your car.

The deep darkness beyond is where I have to go, until I find someone kind enough to help me.

But my hand is just stuck on the gearshift. I never learned to drive in daylight. How am I expected to do it at night?

A freezing air rushes through my lungs and pins me to the back of the seat. My chest punches the steering wheel, and the horn blares like an angry monster.

A vengeful scream tears across my mind.

"AAAAHHHHHHHHHHHHHHH!!!"

Sawyer is not dead yet. Sawyer is back inside my body—

My hand pushes the stick back to park.

—and my body can't decide who to trust.

My head slams into the window, like it's on punishment from itself. My fingers curl around the handle and open the door.

I slide off the seat. A *SMACK* on the asphalt. The door warning is beeping and beeping, cutting through the silence of the woods.

This road, where not a single car is driving, will silence my demise. Not one person will see what happens here tonight. No one will know until morning if this demon rips my body in half.

This road is full of the tiny pieces of rock that didn't fuse properly with the paving. It cuts me up all over as I crawl forward—toward what, I don't know. Barf explodes from my mouth, coloring the road's yellow lines in reddish brown. Up the road, up the road, and I swallow spit, my elbows and knees scraping open little by little.

I detach.

My soul peels up from my body, and then I'm bathed in light, floating inches off the ground, backward and upward. I don't feel right. My throat is dry, my stomach concave, my vision blurry.

Lower, I command myself, and float down so my feet meet the ground.

Sawyer, as me, stands up, in full control of my motor functions. All five-foot-nine of Jake Livingston in his St. Clair Prep uniform—red bow tie, gray sweater vest and slacks—is walking like a zombie toward itself. Smiling evilly, limping like a ghoul. The twisted look makes the face nearly unrecognizable.

I don't have any help anymore. River's not here. I have to do this part by myself.

I reach for the ecto-mist, willing it to help me, and it pulls from the spaces in trees, the cracks in the pavement, the inside of crystal rocks, rushing to swim around my hands and arms to promise me strength.

And I start my dance—whipping my arms around my body as my ancestors ground me in gravity and follow my movements. Energy bolts through my shoulders, lungs, chest, hands. I fire the energy at my body in a blast,

It hits the chest of the dummy Jake, and he flies through space, hitting his back on the asphalt, leaving Sawyer as a legless torso floating aimlessly above him.

I close my eyes and vortex into my skin, facing whiplash as my real eyes open to a star-filled sky.

I spring off my hands and knees, thrashing through Sawyer and toward the truck. These moments, where I'm synched with my body, soul, and mind, are so rare.

I dive in through the door and grab the kerosene off the passenger-side floor. My arm twists behind my back, and my legs sweep from underneath me.

I slam the pavement with my ribs and chin as Sawyer's scream tears through my mind:

RELAX.

I pull down the asphalt, gripping the kerosene so hard my nails dig into my palm around the handle. My neck cracks like a crisp lobster. My head picks up the grime of the road, as if it wants to get dirty, and pain explodes through my network of bones.

I remember . . . in the bathroom, I tore through his being with the strength of my will.

You can beat him, comes a whisper through the darkness, an echo of assurance from the ecto-mist. It glows above my knuckles and fastens there, like weapons of glittering blue brass. *Fight,* it whispers—a choir of voices in perfect harmony.

I use my free arm to pull myself farther down the road.

"GET OUT!!!" The words erupt madly.

Gunshots explode through my brain and flash white across my vision, and through the noise, a thought is forming, like a stage whisper.

Circle, it says. *Circle, circle, circle, circle, circle . . .*

"A circle," I respond.

A circle, they command. *Close, close, close, close . . . close the circle.*

I don't ask questions. The mist has never guided me wrong, and it never would. I get on my knees and skid across the twinkling rocks in the blacktop, spilling the kerosene in a circle.

CIRCLE . . . CIRCLE . . . CIRCLE.

Glug-glug-glug-glug-glug—the clear fluid spatters out of the bottle.

The ground rips from underneath me, and my body is tossed into the air, catching itself horizontally, five feet off the ground. The kerosene hits the road and continues to spill out.

And then my body is falling, pulling my soul out of its skin.

I am a soul again, floating, and watching from above as my body hits the asphalt and the breath leaves my lungs. In a glide toward the wobbly earth of dead world, I land on my fingers and toes outside the kerosene circle.

My physical body lifts itself behind me, charges forward— furious and determined under Sawyer's control.

Kill him. The mist pulses around my hands like rings of magic, offering its power. *Kill him.*

I raise my hands in defense, and a surge of power runs up the veins in my arms and explodes from the center of my chest. A cannon of pink and blue light obliterates my physical self into a cluster of stars.

And in those stars, Sawyer separates from my body like apple skin ripping off the fruit.

And my body—it flies like a paper airplane backward through the air, landing on its back, outside of the circle.

Sawyer doesn't turn around for it. So focused on killing my soul, he rises like a phoenix in front of me. Red flares roar around him in the shape of tortured faces and curled fingers, all reaching out and obscuring the shape of him. He rips his throat open, and the wraith hands lunge for me.

I block them with a field of ecto-mist, which rises like a wall from the concrete. As it falls, it forms a standing shape of blue dust and red smoke, all of it melting into solid colors and textures—a light blue diner dress, a blond-haired head. A woman with a tote bag strung over her shoulder, holding a gun. The weapon is both there and escaping through the night like bubbles in seltzer. I lift my arm, lifting her with me. She's only a wraith of my creation—a puppet attached to my string.

But Sawyer's eyes widen in fear—his face is of a scared child as he floats down to the ground. His feet sink slightly into the asphalt. His body is curled back and fearful, like a baby deer in front of a speeding truck.

I thrust energy out of my chest-arm network and through the wraith of his mother, sending a perfect slice of blinding ecto-mist through his mother's arm in a bomb-shaped bullet. It hits Sawyer hard in the chest, blasts through his heart, and blows him backward. Then he's frozen in midair: one leg bent upward, an arm twisted behind his back, head wrenched toward one shoulder, chest aimed at the sky.

Mist particles stampede his veins, eating him from the inside out as the mother conjuring melts away. The skin of his cheeks sinks under the jawbones, and he rots as strings of ecto-mist deepen in his throat, choking him.

I saw something in that moment . . . There was a Sawyer that didn't realize he'd become a mass shooter, one who maybe wouldn't have if somebody had stepped in sooner.

But now there's a decaying spirit, a harmful person who chose to play parasitic leech, to suck joy out of people and kill everyone it could until it met its match.

I—Jake Livingston—am Sawyer Doon's match.

I run around the circle and find my scrawny body curled like an S.

I fall through my skin, and reality pangs through me like a gong. Fierce sensations come back—damp asphalt, blinding headlights, thrumming engine, and the aches. Aches in my elbows and knees.

I touch the lighter to the wet asphalt. Fire erupts and travels in an arc around the dying Sawyer, forming a full circle. Scooting backward from the insane heat, sweat spills down my neck, clavicles, and chest.

Sawyer pulls at the mist chain around his neck, but it's too strong for him. His body chips away as the termites of stars make him their victim. Ecto-mist insects burrow under his skin, weakening every part of him. His hair—wispy string. His arms—strips of thread. A concert of noise from the mist—screaming, whips, gunfire. Horses, dogs, police sirens.

"Sawyer Doon." My voice is, at first, a polite mutter, directed at the unrecognizable thing hanging in the ring of fire. "I banish you." From the dredges of the fight left in me, I scream it at the top of my lungs, expelling it into the heat waves. "I BANISH YOU FROM LIFE AND MEMORY, FOREVER. *I BANISH YOU TO DEATH.*"

A red line rips across Sawyer's neck. Out spills bloody smoke, and then a mop of fuzzy hair, and then a full head. Skeletal fingers wedge his skin open. A full wraith—no, a soul—bursts from his neck, leaping up into the smoke, shrieking and vanishing.

Sawyer no longer has the means to pull it back. Another breaks free—an entire digested human spirit, this one with blackish hair. And another, until it's a stream of bodies climbing out of Sawyer's neck, tumbling upward like floating roses set on fire. The mist gathers in the open space at his throat, filling it, forcing a gurgle from his mouth.

It invades the gaps of his eyes, popping them out like marbles. Sawyer is frail and eyeless, and his jaw cracks open and hangs off, like a cadaver in shock.

A final creature, unlike the others, claws its way out of his mouth, its hands and teeth built of black smoke—the matter of death. It crawls down Sawyer's body and bleeds like ash from his feet into the ground. And then the ash forms a circle of glowing dust, which fuses slowly together into something new.

A hand breaks from the asphalt like the arm of Satan himself, grabbing on to Sawyer's shriveled-up ankle. In that connection, new matter begins to form—a foot, a new leg, fusing with the fallen wraith, rebuilding it in the shape of a gray foot with webbed toes. Sawyer's other foot nub sprouts more bone by itself, as if a growth agent has spread through his body. His left leg grows and places itself on the ground as a solid. His fingers glue themselves together, fusing into a single tendon.

I back away from the monster as it coalesces before me, as sharp teeth—stalactites and stalagmites—snake out from the gums and wrap around the head.

A new structure of a head arrives where the hair burned off—a bald head.

Gray skin. No eyes. A cave of teeth. Double my size, with a quarter of my strength.

Sawyer, the ghoul.

It rears its head and roars at the moon. The forest stirs from the tormented noise as the mist blows away. Wings flap and rodents skitter, as if every animal on earth has been stirred.

The creature keels over, clawing at its face, and backs to the edge of the fire, toward the forest.

A warrior of ecto-mist charges from the wood at the same time. A woman with hair that covers one half of her face and drapes around her like a glittering silk. Not a woman . . . a girl.

Crawling forward to get a closer look, I realize the shoulder positioning, the way they're hunched forward, the hands and long fingers, the skull at the center of her shirt. It looks like . . . It looks like River.

River, a god of ecto-mist, unwraps a ring of rope from around her arm and lassos it around the ghoul's neck, like a leash. She yanks the monster so it lands with a *THUD* and drags it off the road, into the black of the forest.

The creature's thrashing creates a contrast to her calm, and the tortured howl carries on, rushing through the pines.

Gradually, it quiets, distancing itself, until finally . . . it dies completely.

I'm left alone on the road, hunched over my bloodied knuckles, staring into the softening flame.

No ghosts.

No phantoms.

No ghouls.

No wraiths.

No Sawyer.

Just me.

But Sawyer will be out there as something different now. He'll be the fear in the corners of kids' bedrooms. The monster staring grieving parents in the face.

I push myself up and hobble toward the Tahoe, with the cracked windshield and crinkled-up hood. Inside, I slam the door, causing crystals of broken glass to rain into my lap.

With trembling hands, I lift my phone from my pocket, blood from my finger spreading across the screen as I dial Benji.

He answers after one ring. "Jake, what the fuck? Where did you go?"

"Sending my location," I choke out. "Please come." I'm starting to sob. "Please hurry."

My phone slips, and my head hits the wheel. Tears tremble in my throat and shake down my body as I pick up the phone and send my brother my location.

"Jake?" he calls. "Hello?"

Thunder bowls across the sky, and then the rain starts, hard, as if to wash it all away.

To give me a new start.

It's over. It's over.

"Please come." I drop the phone in my lap and then rest my head against the wheel, quickly losing consciousness. "Please...."

JAKE

I wake up in a bed, in a room that's not mine.

Or anybody's. It's a hospital bed. There's tubing attached to my chest and head. There's a TV on the wall and a pyramid of coffee cups stacked on the table by the window.

Benji is in a chair by the bed. "Thank God," he says when I come to. "What happened to you?"

It's just us in here, and that old cat-and-mouse cartoon on TV.

"Where's Mom?" I ask.

"She went to the bathroom."

"I killed him . . . I . . . I finally killed him." The words fall out like a rockslide, and then I remember who I'm talking to. "You'd never believe it."

The white blankets over my legs feel like they're defeating me, even though I won. In some ways, I will always be ostracized from my family, and I just have to learn to accept it.

Benji says, "I believe you."

I wonder at first if it's a joke. *No criticism? No mocking?*

He's serious. His expression is soft, his eyes open to listen.

"Why didn't you believe me earlier?"

"I don't know. Your life doesn't make sense to me. But I guess it doesn't have to make sense for it to be real. Like, what do I look like, going around telling people my brother sees dead people?"

"I know. You have to fit in."

He cuts his eyes at me. "And so do you. Sometimes I do the most, but you don't do enough. We both have our ways."

It's true. I've always shied away from challenging the white people at school when I don't do what they want me to. But Benji rises to it. Maybe his influence brought me to where I could stand up to my bully.

"Anyway, what's going on with you is too fucking crazy not to believe something's different at this point," he says. "Hard not to notice when you go from staying in your room all day to being paranoid about everything, stealing the car, crashing it. Like, this ain't you. None of it. And even if it was the ghost, I'm glad one of you decided to fight me back. I needed that."

I can't figure out what to say next. *Thank you? You're welcome?* I'm grateful for this moment, but it feels so foreign, like Benji is speaking a new language.

"You kind of fucked up the Tahoe," he says. "I hope you have money for repairs."

Oh, shit. "Is Mom mad?"

"Just worried and confused. But she'll be glad you're awake."

I still enjoy stuff like the cartoon that's playing, along with animated movies and stuff aimed at kids. I wonder if Benji put it on because he knew I would want to see it as I woke up. I always feel like I'm learning slower than everyone around me what exactly I'm supposed to like and how I'm supposed to be.

"Benji?" I say.

"Yeah?"

"I'm gay."

He nods. "Yes. You are."

"You knew?"

"Yes, everybody knows." He smiles and blinks, not mocking, but not concerned with it either. "I'm glad almost dying in the middle of a road has given you the courage to say it."

"I can't be *that* gay."

"Nah, you're pretty gay."

I never wanted to hide who I was until I was told to. I bought the magazine because even if the world wasn't ready to take me seriously, I was ready to take myself seriously as a member of the LGBTQ+ community.

When Dad was beating me up and Mom was watching, Benji came downstairs, I guess to see what was going on. He watched too, for a few seconds. And then he jumped in, grabbed my dad's arms, and stopped him. Dad screamed at him to get off, but Benji persisted and pushed him away from me, forming an open path for me to escape.

"Jake, get out!" he shouted before my dad knocked the blood from my brother's gums.

They stumbled around the living room, and I escaped through the kitchen.

I ran and cried and regretted the day I was born, until finally I fell asleep on the swings of our neighborhood park, clinging to particles of rain condensation for comfort.

There are many things about life I've yet to understand, because some resist clear definitions. Like Benji, who's always been easy for me to call a train wreck. A rebel with no cause. A bully whose shadow I never wanted to live in because I didn't want people thinking I was like him.

But Benji is the same guy who saved my life when I needed it most.

He's the one who stood up for me in the moment it really mattered.

I start crying. I can't stop it. Sometimes things get too big for me to understand, and it overwhelms me. He's not judging me for it.

"I don't want people to realize I'm gay, though," I whisper.

"But you are." He puts his hand on mine, which is trapped under the cover. "And it doesn't matter. At the end of the day, you can't change yourself. So you have no choice but to be yourself. Fuck everyone who has a problem with it. You're still a man."

"Okay."

"Say it."

"I'm . . . still a man?"

"And Dad is a dickhead."

"And Dad is a dickhead."

"And if anyone has shit to say about you, you just do them like you did Chad and keep it moving. We'll handle the charges later."

I chuckle through my tears. Even if he's wrong and that advice would get me into a lot of trouble, there's something to be said for having someone around who takes the risk without considering the consequence. Who does what he wants because he wants to.

I admit it. There's something to be said for my brother.

"Thank you for listening to me for once in your life."

To that, he smirks and rolls his eyes. "Yeah, whatever. Don't get used to it. At school on Monday I won't know who you are."

"That's okay with me. I have better friends now."

"Finally—God. So, I'm gonna give Mahalia this." He cracks open a black box from his book bag to reveal a necklace with a diamond pendant. "As I explain that demons have been haunting our lives and that's why—"

"That's why you cheated on her? Because of demons?"

"Okay . . . I'm still framing the story. But there *was* a demon in our house, right?"

"I think you have to just treat her better, be a better person, and not cheat on her anymore. That's the only thing that will win her back."

"Okay, I'm asking you what your queer eyes think of the necklace, not for your judgment on my relationships. Jesus."

"Did you steal it?"

"No, dummy—I bought it."

"In that case . . . it's very pretty."

"Success." He frowns at my head, the turban of gauze wrapped around it. "Damn, that ghost really fucked your shit up, huh?"

I see a flash of hot blood exploding from Rod's body, under a spray of bullets. I feel the smoke of his burning house roaring up my throat.

"Can we talk about it later?" I ask.

He hesitates some. "Okay."

For now I'm at peace, and I'd like to hold on to this moment. I close my eyes and take in the sounds of the animated show. The *zips* and *zoinks* and *boings!*

It was the closest I'd come to violence before stabbing someone and then shooting someone else and setting his body on fire. I could have saved his life had I fought back sooner. Could have accessed the power I knew was inside me, but I decided it wasn't worth it.

One day, I hope, I'll be able to live with that. One day I'll forget that I was able to kill a man.

JAKE

When I was asleep, I had an experience.

There was total darkness, and then ecto-mist was expanding beneath me like a field of electric dandelion petals. A sky broke out above in shades of vibrant purple and pink, and then I found River, now a constellated figure, approaching me from across the ecto-field.

"Funny seeing you here," she said.

Then we were standing right across from each other. I looked at my arms and found them outlined in the astral glow. "Does this mean we'll only get to see each other when I have a near-death experience?"

She pondered it for a moment. "I think that's how the full-body thing works. But you can hear me at all times."

"In the mist."

"In the mist. I visited my mom. Could swear she heard me while she was doing dishes. She put her head toward the curtains like they were whispering to her, and she said my name."

"I'm glad you got in touch. And thank you. I don't think I could've stopped him without . . ." I gestured at the ecto-mist floating around us like sedated smoke fairies. "All this. Thank you."

"Thank you. This place does feel better than where I was before. Stuck in that room, I felt like that was it. Death was this horrible loop I'd have to live in, and peace after it didn't exist. But here, all I feel is peace. Here, I hear the voices of everyone I care about at exactly the moment they think of me. I hear them instead of him." River looked at their hands and cheesed at the crystals and diamonds shining in them. "It's really cool, honestly."

It got me thinking about the dead world as a haven of possibilities rather than a hopeless nightmare. "Now that we've joined bodies and made that connection, do you think we'll have a telepathic connection forever?"

"Would be cool," she said. "Inter-realm friendship. But I hope it's not because we joined bodies, but because we just remember each other. Because if it's the body joining that secures the telepathy, then that means you-know-who will be in your head forever too."

There was a tremor at the mention of him, and then a guttural roar exploded somewhere in the darkness.

"Where did you take him?" I asked.

"To hell," River said. "Where his ass belongs. I think you were meant to find me. We were meant to team up to take this kid out. Can I ask for a favor, medium?"

"Anything."

"Now that I've had a lot more time to think about final words, I want to get a message to my mom once and for all. One that convinces her I wrote it while I was here, and she's just finding it."

"I can do that. What would you say?"

✛

The first day I'm discharged from the hospital, I open my sketchpad on my desk and begin to write under an exhausted orange sunlight, which spills through the blinds and over my battered knuckles. It's like her words are imprinted into my own mind as things I said once upon a time—instantly memorable.

Dear Mom,

It's easier to say this in writing.

I never feel right telling the people I love the most I love them. I don't know why. Maybe I just know you'll always be there for me, so it's easiest to give you the worst parts of me, knowing they'll be forgiven.

But I'm choosing to say it now. I love you more than anything, in spite of everything happening now, and despite whatever happens later. I love you, forever.

The way you fight for me encourages me to fight for myself. I'm fighting for myself because you fought for me. I'm fighting for other people I love because you fought for me.

I know we never agreed on religion. But I believe in connections that transcend material reality too. I believe that if I lose you, or if you lose me, we'll still be with each other. And that death is not always an ending. Sometimes it's a beginning, and for lots of us, life continues, no matter what form your body takes.

I like to think that if I die, I'll still be with you, even when you can't see me. I hope we can agree to believe in that together.

Love always,

River

At one p.m., I take my bike to River's home at 452 Dhalgren Way. There's a beauty to the little houses behind Heritage's colonial front. Bungalows and huts in vibrant colors—pinks and yellows—balled up in the trees like the gemstones in Ms. Josette's shop, each with its own character and purpose.

A mosaic globe in a flowerpot sits in the middle of the lawn like a mirror ball reflecting the universe.

River lived in a yellow house with a porch and rocking chair. Begonias, orchids, and ferns hang from the porch, their plants green and healthy like little rain forests bursting with life, ecto-mist whispering through their stems when the wind blows.

I find the key in the garden's fake rock like she told me and tiptoe into her house, up to her room. A jumble of black- and pink-themed stuff. Posters for campy slashers, flowers that have wilted and are hanging upside down on the wall. Flowers that are fresh, surrounding a picture of her on the dresser. It's in the middle of candles and cards.

I find her journal, all black with a silver clasp, amid a shelf of records—Death Grips, Shygirl, the Smiths. I slip the letter in the back, letting the paper stick out just a little. Her family will find it eventually.

✛

When the doctors asked me, "What made you lose control of the vehicle?" I didn't say anything. Mom sat in the chair at the foot of the bed, and all I saw was her hair.

There is dark imagery bleeding and frying in the tortured trap of my mind. Rod's body on that floor. I have to bury it and forget it happened, just so I can keep going.

It takes a few days after I leave the hospital for home to finally feel somewhat safe. The kitchen is quiet, but I always imagine someone dead on the floor. The bathroom is a bathroom—cold and empty, bug-free. There's solace in the bedroom, except for when I catch a shadow in the corner and turn to find no one there.

Mom doesn't press too much on what happened—I think I'm an explosive bomb in the room whose silence feels a little deadly. I don't blame anyone for not wanting to talk to me. I've never talked much to other people.

⊹

I have text messages from Allister, and Fiona invites me on a low-stress rock-climbing excursion.

On the third day home, I decide I can make that happen and toss all my clothes from my dressers and closet to pick an outfit. I'm so used to being in uniform that I have no idea how to dress for *occasions*. But it's nice not to think about a uniform anymore.

On the bed is a T-shirt from my friend Jalen. His family owned a T-shirt business, and he gave me that for my birthday, with *JJL* printed in bright blue and green graffiti. Jake Joseph Livingston.

I remember my unraveling it from the tissue paper. He said, "Now you have something Black to wear." And laughed. I frowned until he slapped me on the shoulder and said, "Relax! It's a joke. Do whatever you want."

Jalen didn't judge me. I knew he'd never do that, that we'd still see movies together and pass notes in class despite how I talked or what I wore. He liked me for me. He invited me to join basketball games and tackle football in the community yard of my old neighborhood. Even when Benji didn't invite me, he asked where I was. He wanted me to be included.

I never felt equipped for the roughness of the other boys. A tackle was never just a tackle. It was a bum-rush, a blunt-force blow to the head, an occasional broken bone, which we'd shrug off and realize later.

But Jalen I felt comfortable with, because he was nice to me.

Too nice. I got the dumb impression he'd be okay if I asked if he "liked me" or "*liked me* liked me." And after that, he didn't invite me out anymore, didn't even ask about me, didn't even look at me.

So no one asked about me. I remember watching movies about gay people, white gay people, because that's what was most available. I scoured the library for more books about white gay people. I assumed there'd be people who'd accept me for me eventually, and I'd just not found them yet.

I stare at the custom-made shirt and get lost staring at it.

"*I don't roll that way, bruh.*" I hear his voice even when I don't want to—the intonation, the dismissiveness. I hear the atmosphere of the hallway he said it in, the audience of kids who may not have heard him. It jumps out in memory as the moment my heart first broke.

Allister, I hope you know it's not that I don't like you—it's just that I don't feel safe with anyone.

I wish I could explain why it hurts where it does and how it affects my interactions.

Mom knocks on the door. I know it's her, because her knocks are always soft, like questions, while Benji's are hard, like answers. Her knocks respect my boundaries.

"Come in," I say, wanting to profusely apologize, because I never wanted to do something that a reckless teenager would, like take the car and crash it, or fight at school.

But now, as she leans into the doorway, afraid to come in, I'm not the approachable son she once counted on anymore.

She's smiling, but it's sad and distant. She knows now that not everything about me is soft and gentle and good, and that some things are reckless and violent.

"Are you sure you're ready to get back out there?" she asks. "I mean, your head . . ."

It's been four days of gauze, but today I unwrapped it to expose the red spot, just in the corner of my head, at the hairline.

"Yeah, I'm ready." I finally take a black hoodie off the hanger and throw it over my body.

"Okay, well, don't forget your coat, your hat, and your scarf." Still she speaks like those bad parts are just parts and not the whole picture.

"The hoodie is enough, Mom. Also, I don't own a scarf."

"I'll lend you one of mine—it's supposed to hit the twenties this week."

"Okay." I offer a fake smile, nod, and accept the fact I'll just have to sneak out of the house so she doesn't know I'm not wearing a scarf. Definitely not one of hers.

Mom hesitates a little and looks at me humbly, like there's something big she needs to say.

When I was alone with Benji at the hospital, he said, "I'll tell Mom to chill on questions until you're ready to talk."

It must have worked, because she hasn't really asked. But she still looks like she's been crying a lot and trying her best to hide it.

"I'm sorry, Jake. I don't know what's going on, but I'm sorry for not making it feel like a safe environment. I didn't know it would be this bad for you at St. Clair."

"It's okay. I didn't say anything. I should've."

"Maybe it's not a suitable environment for you, and we can find you a better school."

"Clark High?"

Mom looks unsure. "Are you ready for that?"

"I think so."

I just needed to start owning who I was. That's why I could never function at my district school. People had everything to say about the fact my shoes were dirty.

I didn't know how to let people's opinions of me not matter. But it's pointless to try to change anything about myself, because I can't. Might as well just find people who are okay with it.

My family, as it turns out, has never been as bad as I thought they were.

Mom tries to smile, but it wanes. "I'm sorry I let your father do that to you."

The mention of him drops into the room like a bomb, toxifying the air.

"I should have stepped in. I should have stopped it." And then she's crying. All of a sudden. "I'm sorry if I made you feel like I wasn't there. I spent a lot of years living in fear. Being so used to the routine, the expectation of a traditional family. And now, after twenty years, I feel like I'm stepping into something better. Setting myself free from that. I wish I could've done that before you and Benji got hurt."

This is the first time I've heard any of this. My parents argued all the time before getting divorced. I never saw it happen, but I would hear crashing from their bedroom when they screamed at each other. I'm not the only one Dad was violent with.

And I guess before now, I'd never had a reference to imagine what that feels like. Dad must have preyed on her the way Sawyer preyed on me, in a way that felt completely inescapable and held her back not just from me, but from everything. From life.

There is a world she sees that I don't, and that I never could.

I understand now that I'm not the only one misunderstood.

I forgive her.

We're free now. It feels like we can understand each other better in this environment, undo what my dad did to both of us.

I walk over, wrap her in a hug, and imagine Grandpa smiling somewhere in approval.

"I'm glad you're thinking about what you want now," I tell her. "You're a great mom and deserve that."

Her eyes well with tears. I don't think she hears that enough.

My phone vibrates, and I pull it from my pocket to find a text from Fiona. *Outside!*

⁘

I've never seen anything like a rock-climbing gym.

After we check in, we drop our bags into lockers, and Fiona leads me through the place. I rotate my head around the high walls, taking it all in. It's like a cave built by a professional painter. Big sky-blue walls, with grips like floating orbs. They remind me of my ancestors, solid, unbreakable, the grips like the organs in their bodies.

Fiona leads us down some low tunnels and alcoves, away from the center of the gym and into a section of smaller walls, which you don't need ropes or a harness to climb.

"We're not climbing the big ones?" I ask.

"I like how free these feel," she says. "I like not being held back by the ropes."

Every climbing sequence is color-coded and rated between 5.0 and 5.15, telling you how difficult they'll be. Fiona climbs the 5.8's, and I start lower, with the 5.2's.

Fiona sits on the mat as I climb, clapping and cheering me on. Every time I come to a grip that seems too far for me to reach and I feel like falling, she shouts, "Come on! You can do it, Jake." Like it's a matter of fact. "Just grab it."

So I just grab it. And then I grab the next one, and I realize my brain is what's been limiting me all along. My legs move as my arms do, as I stretch to full capacity.

To take every risk.

To beat any fear.

We break for lunch around some benches and tables, away from the mats. Sub sandwiches and chips that we picked up from a deli on the way here. The turkey and cheese on my sub is refreshing and hearty. It has a perfect dash of lettuce and tomato to hit the veggie food group; now that I'm athletic, I'm trying to eat healthier.

Across the mats I spot a ghoul sitting cross-legged behind a brown boy being attached to a harness by his mother. Humans phase through it like it isn't even there, because it isn't. It has no power to touch you until you're already dead.

I swallow sandwich and gulp down water and tell Fiona, "Allister told me he has a crush on me."

I half expect the world to end, for ghouls and gods to break out into battle among the mats of the climbing gym, zombie titans and misty knights clashing swords and limbs.

Fiona's not shocked by the reveal. Her eyebrows are lifting higher and higher with intrigue. "Well, that's good news," she says, and then tries to gauge my reaction. "Right?"

I shrug in agreement.

Fiona nods, like she's known it all along, and takes another bite of her sub. "I see it on you guys," she says, mouth half-full. "I figured there was something up."

"You did?"

"Duh, you're practically holding hands. In spirit, at least. If there were auras, your auras would be holding hands, you know? Great chemistry."

I can't help but laugh, because it's literally true. "Our auras definitely hold hands."

Weird how nervous I was to tell her. Fiona's never seemed homophobic, but maybe I thought she'd only like me if our relationship went to the next level. It's clear now she never wanted that. Fiona is cool just being an awesome friend.

"So, are you *officially* dating?" Fiona asks, excitement building in her voice.

"I haven't given him an answer. I kind of just garbled some words and disappointed him."

"Well, let me know when you finally go for it, because I'm happy to lend you my car if you want to be the one to pick him up. I know all that is far into the future, but planning *is* a virtue in some cases."

I don't know why I want to laugh. Maybe because the boy climbing the wall has reached the top, touched the big button, and now he's screaming with excitement at himself. A chorus of strangers cheers for him as the ropes lower him to the ground, where he meets his smiling mother again.

Fiona didn't judge me for stabbing Chad. In fact, she said he deserved it, and she's glad I stood up for myself, despite how the school punished me as a result.

"I really like you, Fiona."

Her face lights up. "I like you too, Jake." She laughs modestly at her lap.

I'm going to try to say things more as they occur to me. To turn my positive thoughts into positive energy.

I'm glad I came out to her, but I'm still afraid of what happens next. What will Mom think? Can I walk into a room and just say it out loud, and not fear what might happen? It still doesn't feel all the way comfortable. But I owe it to myself to stand up to things that scare me, and I'll get there.

After we gobble down the lunch, we go back to the walls. She's happy to have me here, getting into something she's passionate about. I can tell by her aura, which waves behind her as she starts to climb, in a cape of yellows, blues, and greens. Like the sky, the ocean, and the earth.

I gear up for a more intermediate level—a 5.6—and get to climbing. Stuck in the middle, the next grip reveals itself to me, farther than I think I can reach.

"You got this, Jake!" Fiona calls behind me.

And for once in my life, I believe it.

JAKE

ME: Hey, can we see each other soon?

ALLISTER: Glad to see you're,
um... alive! Lol.

ME: Sorry to leave you hanging.
Lots to explain.

ALLISTER: I have a lot of time.

ME: So, when are you free?

ALLISTER: Like I said, I have a lot
of time.

ME: Time in general, or time for me?

ALLISTER: Time for you. I do have a
life, you know. But yes, if you want to
talk, I would love to listen.

ME: Sorry to just ghost you for days.

ALLISTER: You apologize too much.
You have a life too.

ME: I know. Trying not to be so
sorry for everything.

ALLISTER: So, where's it gonna be?
You pick the place. I picked the last
place.

ME: ...

ALLISTER: Make up your mind, Jake!
No more indecisiveness!

ME: Do you like burgers?

ALLISTER: Love them.

ME: How about Infinity Burger
in Little Five Points?

ALLISTER: Count me in. What time?

ME: ...

ALLISTER: Now? Sounds great! Just
need to shower and get dressed. Be
there in an hour.

⁜

Infinity Burger is as any good burger joint should be. The walls
are covered in license plates, old advertisements, and photo-
graphs of icons from the past—actors and musicians.

I get there first and slide into a booth, where I wait for five,
ten, and then fifteen minutes, picking at my nails and leaving
shavings on the checkerboard tablecloth.

What if he stands me up? What if he hates me for the way I responded before and this is his revenge?

He lied when he said he'd arrive in an hour, because he's twenty minutes late.

I get why, though. He's looking gorgeous as he approaches the table, in clothes that feel a lot older than we are—skinny jeans, leather boots, a bomber jacket. Of course he cleans up nice. And here I am in my same busted sneakers, jeans that barely fit, and a hoodie.

He slides into the booth across from me, and I'm rendered speechless by the way his skin glows under the light fixture dangling between us. There are silver crystals in his ears, which I didn't even realize were pierced. I like that. Among everything else.

"Damn," he says, suppressing a smile. "Thought we'd get to spend a little bit more time together before you went and got yourself suspended."

I roll my eyes and bury my face in my hands. "Please shut up. Oh my God."

He lets out the laughter he was holding in, flashing that beautiful smile. "No, I think it was badass. Everyone I've talked to says that guy was a dick and had it coming."

"Yeah, no kidding. A big one."

"A big dick?" Allister picks up the glass of ice water on the table and gulps down half of it, surveying the restaurant with his eyes as if he didn't just say that.

I'm so into him, I consider sitting across a table from him a blessing. Despite the fact he drinks straight out the glass in public restaurants, which is something I'd never do.

"I think we'll get to the dick part later?" I say. "Pretty sure that's how it works, not that I've ever done it before."

He slams the glass down and lifts his eyebrows. At first, I think I've gone too far, but then I process his emotion. He looks kind of . . . impressed?

The waiter comes to our table just in time to spare me further embarrassment. I hope I didn't say something wrong in the pursuit of saying things that feel right.

The waiter introduces himself to Allister as Kenny and asks for our orders. I order the Mushroom Madness burger, which I'd been poring over the menu to decide on for fifteen minutes, torn between dozens of tempting descriptions.

But Allister doesn't bother even looking at it. All he says is, "Surprise me." And hands both menus to the waiter, not giving him a choice.

Kenny hesitates. "Ummm . . ."

"I trust you, sir," Allister says. "I eat everything that tastes good, and your tattoos already prove you have impeccable taste."

Allister's charm rises off his aura in bubbles of red, white, and rosy pink. Kenny looks down at his colorful sleeve of tattoos—where cartoon characters and symbols are etched into his skin—and he has no choice but to smile.

"Thanks, that's nice of you," he says. "Hope I don't disappoint you."

After he wanders off, I roll my eyes at Allister. "Always a charmer."

"Life's not worth it if you're a dud." He puts both elbows on the table and leans toward me. "So, where were we? Dicks."

"Maybe we should rewind? I haven't even responded to your confession yet."

"If you tell me that you invited me here to break my heart, I'm storming out."

"Actually, I invited you here to tell you that I like you back."

A smile spreads across his face. "Of course you do," he says. "Who wouldn't?"

"Oh, Lord . . ."

He laughs, and I laugh with him.

"But I might be changing schools," I say, sucking the joy from the moment.

He looks bummed. And then he nods, takes a breath, and smiles. I just watched him be sad and transform his sadness into okayness. Glee, even. I guess that's his special ability.

"I'll work around not being able to stare at the back of your head in psych," he says. "But if we won't be seeing each other, you can't ghost my texts anymore."

"Ghost . . . was that a pun?"

"Of course, thanks for noticing."

"Of course. Anyways . . ." It's my turn to take a deep breath, and with it, I take in the air of the place, an air of TV screens, car bumpers, beer, sports and blue jeans and life. "I won't ghost your texts. I'm trying to be a better communicator or whatever."

"Good. Talking to the dead is not enough."

"I'm not even good at that, though, which is the real tragedy."

Allister lilts his head in agreement. "Yeah, that's not looking great for you. I mean, it's kind of like oral and written communication skills—you really need one or the other to have a strong résumé."

"Thanks for rubbing it in."

"In this house, we only deal in facts. What, would you prefer I lied to you?"

"Never. The main reason I like you is *because* you're real."

I grab a salt packet from its little house of salt on the table, rip it open, and spill it across the wood surface.

"Are we making contact with Satan now?" Allister asks as I run my fingers through it.

"No, I just think it's cool to draw with salt."

Allister clicks his tongue and then rolls it around his mouth. I'm noticing his tongue is really very intriguing—redder than usual, like a tangy cherry.

He looks around the joint, at the girls in their dresses and jeans, all with some dramatic tattoos—snakes and spiders. His eyes land on me again as he picks up his water for a sip. "What do you think ol' Kenny's gonna bring me back from the kitchen?"

"Probably the fried chicken burger."

Allister snickers mid-sip and catches the falling water in his hand. "I was in the middle of a sip, you bitch." He yanks a napkin from its dispenser and wipes away his sparkle of saliva and ice water. "I want my Kool-Aid in a wineglass, or else."

"Or else you'll lay everybody the fuck out." I'm laughing through the words.

"Period. Every last one."

And then we're laughing together until our food arrives—not the fried chicken, as it would turn out. Something with bacon and a sweet jelly sauce that Allister calls "delightful!"

He orders me a milkshake, and I twirl it around until it loses its texture. "If you don't drink that, it'll drink you."

So I take the straw out, leave it on a napkin, and chug the whole thing, then slam down the cup.

"Did that bring you joy?" he asks.

I feel about five pounds heavier. "A lot, actually."

This is a really bad time to be noticing more things to love about him, like his left eyebrow, with the faint bald line through it that communicates a world of emotion I've yet to discover.

The bill comes. Allister pays and leaves Kenny a ten-dollar tip.

I have one question when we burst from the doors. "Do you get an allowance?"

"I steal my parents' money." He taps his pockets, I guess to make sure everything is all there.

"And they're okay with you stealing from them?"

"Does it matter?" he says with the friendliest smile I could imagine. "You were paid for, right?"

The sidewalks are aglow from neon restaurant signs and string lights. It's almost too quaint to be true. It takes everything in me not to press my body into his. I feel like the farther we walk, the closer our pinkies get to locking, and if I had it my way, I'd just hold his hand and nobody would stare at us at all, because we'd exist in our own universe.

The sidewalks here are so traversable. It would be a nice place to live together, if it came to that.

"I like the way you talk," I tell him, and to myself, "I'm still learning how to do that."

He swings around a streetlamp, shouts, "Yes!" to the night, as if for no other reason but to shout, to use his voice and his body. And I agree that we should do that more often.

He lands back in step with me. "So, tell me . . . What was the reason you left me hanging when I first told you?"

"I guess it was hard to believe someone like you could like someone like me."

He balks at me and stops, like what I said was ridiculous. "Wait a minute. You're an amazing guy, Jake—stop it."

I stop and turn to face him, immediately wanting to fight the kind words. But I know Allister won't take denial of my greatness for an answer. So I shut up.

"Say thank you, or else," he says.

"Thank you, or else."

"You're annoying."

Around the corner from a pizzeria, where smells of Italian meat and seasonings are wafting from the windows, Allister grabs me by the hand and pulls me down a dark alley.

He leads me over a glistening puddle and toward the dead end. "Your parents know about you?" he asks.

"Not exactly. Yours?" I check behind me to make sure no one's following us and that the dead end is really a dead end and not a drop through dead world into some other century.

"Not exactly."

This could still all be a dream. Or maybe, for once, it's real, and temporarily perfect, and nothing terrible will come next.

I let my hand fold down so it locks through his fingers, and my heartbeat accelerates.

We're holding hands. We're holding hands.

Then I realize what he was walking toward—a dusky orange glow beaming from a light stuck in the mortar.

His cheekbones look soaked in a beach sunset as he cups his thumb in front of my ear, his fingers behind my head. He pulls his face closer to mine, so that the only thing left to do is what I've wanted to do ever since I first saw him. We kiss, and I grab on to his jaw, drawing him in.

We break apart suddenly and look at each other. It's almost like we should fight. Or kiss harder?

We decide on the latter and rush back together. It's an excited, open-lipped kiss, with tongue and the intoxicating flavor of menthol.

He tears his lips off mine, and I trip sideways, but he catches me, interrupting the danger with his safety.

He throws me lightly into the wall for support, and the bricks knock the air to the front of my lungs.

"You okay?" he asks.

"Yeah. I'm great."

"Do you like stuff like that?"

"Honestly, yes."

Allister grins as he licks the taste off his lips, pulls out lip balm, and applies it. All I want is his lips. So I go for it—a third kiss. In this one I put my hands on his chest, and around his neck, because I like how that feels.

Let someone see. Let someone jump out of the darkness and kill me. If there's anything I'd want to be doing on a loop forever, it's this.

It's like everything that came before doesn't matter anymore, and everything that comes next won't either, because his mouth and our hands around each other trap me in a moment, a rush. Like the jolt I get after an astral glide, when my body reminds my soul that it's alive.

ACKNOWLEDGMENTS

⟡

To Rena Rossner, thank you for lifting me out of the query trenches and taking a chance on this offbeat story. Stacey Barney, thank you for challenging me to take my world to new heights. Michael Bourret, thank you for your friendship, your advocacy, and for believing in what I have to say. Thank you to Corey Brickley for creating such an unforgettable cover illustration, and to the entire team at Penguin for your enthusiasm about my work.

Thank you to Rachel Gurevich and Sarah Summerbell for being my first beta readers. To my high school besties, Alessandro Miccio and Aliki Fornier, thank you for giving me a place to be my truest self when I needed it most. Shout-out to Diego, Mia, Ludi, Kyle, Jessi, and Botai for making my college years a lot less hellish than they would've been without you.

To my uncles Bruce and Brent, thank you for loving my first self-published book and inspiring me to keep writing. Thank you to Mom and Grande for reading my early books when I was afraid to show them to anyone else and for giving me the tools I would need to make my dream come true. David, thank you for your enthusiasm for this concept, for keeping me down to earth, and for being a great brother.

Shout-out to my queer Black writer friends Pheolyn Allen, Jamar Perry, Lachelle, and Anthony Isom Jr. for inspiring me with your words, holding me down through the years, and understanding where I'm coming from.

To the creative writing and poetry professors at Hofstra, I appreciated the opportunity to learn from you. Huge thank-you to my first writing teacher, Rosemary McClellan, for telling me I'd be a great writer and for championing me through the publication of my debut.

Thank you to my fellow authors who've gone out of your way to extend any kindness, opportunity, or mentorship: Rita Williams-Garcia, Adam Silvera, Becky Albertalli, Kacen Callender, Amy Reed, Sarah Nicholas, Anica Mrose Rissi, Tom Ryan, Claribel Ortega, Celeste Pewter, Elsie Chapman, Dana Mele, and Rivers Solomon.

And to queer and trans Black people, thank you for your resilience, your magic, and the flavor you bring to the artistic landscape. I'm here because you are.